"Sometimes I Wish I Hadn't Been So Damned Noble."

Rick pulled Lori Lee into his arms, crushing her breasts to his chest, pressing her against him. "I should have taken you with me that night and said to hell with your innocence and with the barriers that stood between us."

Lori Lee pulsated deep in the secret heart of her body. Longings more intense than any she'd ever known radiated through her. "I've always wondered what it would have been like with you."

"I'd have been your first, if I'd taken you that night."

The words were a statement, not a question. All the guys had known that Lori Lee Guy didn't put out, that she was waiting for Prince Charming….

Dear Reader,

A book from Joan Hohl is always a delight, so I'm thrilled that this month we have her latest MAN OF THE MONTH, *A Memorable Man*. Naturally, this story is chock-full of Joan's trademark sensuality *and* it's got some wonderful plot twists that are sure to please you!

Also this month, Cindy Gerard's latest in her NORTHERN LIGHTS BRIDES series, *A Bride for Crimson Falls*, and Beverly Barton's "Southern sizzle" is highlighted in *A Child of Her Own*. Anne Eames has the wonderful ability to combine sensuality and humor, and *A Marriage Made in Joeville* features this talent.

The Baby Blizzard by Caroline Cross is sure to melt your heart this month—it's an extraordinary love story with a hero and heroine you'll never forget! And the month is completed with a sexy romp by Diana Mars, *Matchmaking Mona*.

In months to come, look for spectacular Silhouette Desire books by Diana Palmer, Jennifer Greene, Lass Small and many other fantastic Desire stars! And I'm always here to listen to your thoughts and opinions about the books. You can write to me at the address below.

Enjoy! I wish you hours of happy reading!

Lucia Macro

Lucia Macro
Senior Editor

Please address questions and book requests to:
Silhouette Reader Service
U.S.: 3010 Walden Ave., P.O. Box 1325, Buffalo, NY 14269
Canadian: P.O. Box 609, Fort Erie, Ont. L2A 5X3

BEVERLY BARTON
A CHILD OF HER OWN

SILHOUETTE *Desire*®
Published by Silhouette Books
America's Publisher of Contemporary Romance

SILHOUETTE BOOKS

ISBN 0-373-76077-9

A CHILD OF HER OWN

This edition published by arrangement with Harlequin Books S.A.

® and TM are trademarks of Harlequin Books S.A., used under license. Trademarks indicated with ® are registered in the United States Patent and Trademark Office, the Canadian Trade Marks Office and in other countries.

Printed in U.S.A.

BEVERLY BARTON

has been in love with romance since her grandfather gave her an illustrated book of *Beauty and the Beast*. An avid reader since childhood, she began writing at the age of nine and wrote short stories, poetry, plays and novels throughout high school and college. After marriage to her own "hero" and the births of her daughter and son, she chose to be a full-time home-maker, a.k.a. wife, mother, friend and volunteer.

When she returned to writing, she joined Romance Writers of America and helped found the Heart of Dixie chapter in Alabama. Since the release of her first Silhouette book in 1990, she has won the GRW Maggie Award, the National Readers' Choice Award and has been a RITA finalist. Beverly considers writing romance books a real labor of love. Her stories come straight from the heart, and she hopes that all the strong and varied emotions she invests in her books will be felt by everyone who reads them.

For my daughter, Badiema Beaver Waldrep, and her friend Beth Bange, the two prettiest girls to ever grace the Deshler High School majorette line, and Mandy Hall Files, former lovely DHS drum major.

And a special thanks to my good friend and a lady who, as far as I'm concerned, should always be center stage, Brenda Hall. I appreciate your sharing a hundred and one interesting details with me about your daughter Beth Bange's Quad-Cities Twirlers, National and World Champions.

One

Carrying a steel gray toolbox, Rick Warrick entered the Dixie Twirlers studio and immediately realized half a dozen women were sizing him up. Not that he wasn't used to the fairer sex paying attention to him, but these weren't good-time girls at a local bar. These were wives and mothers, some of them the cream of local society. Glancing around the huge open room, he noticed that the decor was definitely feminine, everything done in various shades of pink and lavender, with gold and silver accents. Surveying the bevy of ladies seated together in a lounge section at the back of the room, he didn't see the studio's owner, Ms. Lori Lee Guy, who had called for a repairman.

His partner, Bobo Lewis, had brought him up-to-date on Lori Lee's life. She was a hometown girl who'd gone to the University of Alabama as a majorette, become homecoming queen and snagged herself a star quarterback. Although he had feigned indifference to Bobo's gossip, Rick had been interested. It wasn't that he'd been carrying a torch for Lori Lee all these years—he hadn't—but he still considered her "the perfect female." He had come to that conclusion when he'd been eighteen and fantasized about scoring with Deshler High School's head majorette. Having seen her recently in passing on the street hadn't changed his opinion.

A hot, jazzy tune drifted down from upstairs, mingling with the sound of dozens of feet tapping and interspersed with childish giggles.

"I'm looking for Ms. Guy," Rick said, not localizing his stare, but taking in all six of the women. "She called about the heat."

A plump redhead dressed in a multicolored sweat suit stood and, swaying her hips provocatively, sauntered over to Rick. "You're Rick Warrick, aren't you? I heard you were back in town and working for Bobo Lewis."

"I'm Bobo's partner," Rick corrected her. He wished it wasn't so important to him for people to know he was more than a hired hand. But dammit, it was important. Because that's all he'd ever been until he'd come home to Tuscumbia and bought half-ownership in Bobo's heating and air-conditioning business. "I'm sorry, ma'am, do we know each other?"

She smiled, deep dimples scoring her round cheeks. "You probably don't remember me from high school. We didn't run in the same circle, but all of us *good* girls had crushes on you." She held out her pudgy hand. Expensive rings adorned several fingers and a diamond tennis bracelet circled her wrist. "I'm Deanie Webber. I used to be Deanie Smith."

Rick couldn't recall the woman, but he admired her honesty and liked her genuinely friendly manner. "It's nice to see you again, Deanie. You must have a kid who takes baton lessons here."

"Yes. She's one of the little darlings upstairs freezing to death," Deanie said. "Twinkle Toes are rehearsing right ow. They're the talented six-to-nine-year-olds. All of us have daughters in the group.''

"I suppose Ms. Guy is up there." Rick nodded toward the staircase.

"Yes, go on up. I don't think they're doing much pracicing. It's too cold." Deanie crossed her arms across her ample bosom and patted herself on her arms. "Lori Lee will be glad to see you. Do you think you can get the heat working soon?"

"I'll give it my best shot once I find the trouble." Rick glanced over Deanie's shoulder at the five other women who were boldly staring at him.

He bounded up the stairs, wanting to escape the ladies' inspection. He heard a buzzing of female voices, the words *bad boy, heartbreaker* and *always in trouble* following his ascent to the second floor.

The second story was a large, open space with a row of windows across the front of the building and well-worn hardwood flooring. Music blared from a jam-box sitting on the wooden floor. Six little girls of various sizes circled their teacher, each child trying to talk at once.

Rick cleared his throat. No one noticed. "Excuse me. I'm A. K. Warrick. I'm here from Lewis Heating and Air."

Suddenly silence claimed the children as all heads turned in Rick's direction. Lori Lee Guy, her hand on a child's shoulder, looked across the room and, for one split second, her heart stopped beating. The black-haired man standing there in his faded jeans, ratty navy sweater and old brown leather jacket took her breath away. Big, tall and badly in need of a shave and a haircut, he dominated the room with his powerful masculine presence.

"Hello," Lori Lee said, amazed that she could speak with her heart caught in her throat. "The heat's not working. It was fine yesterday, but when I came over this afternoon to turn up the thermostat, it wouldn't kick on."

"If you'll show me where the unit is, I'll check it out." Rick tried not to stare too hard. He didn't want to be obvious in his survey, but this was the closest he'd been to her in fifteen years, and he was tempted to drink his fill. She was even more beautiful now than she'd been as a teenager. She was still round and curvy in all the right places. Full breasted, wide hipped, long legged. A trim, hourglass figure. But a mature elegance had replaced her fresh, youthful innocence.

The picture of casual loveliness in her pale blue winter tights and her oversize white mid-thigh sweater, Lori Lee glided across the floor, followed by her pint-size entourage. Her shoulder-length blond ponytail bounced up and down on her back.

"The unit's in the basement, I'm afraid. It'll be even colder down there. I don't know why the heat had to go out the first week in January." Lori Lee paused before she reached Rick's side, turned abruptly, placed her hands on her hips and faced the children. "Go on downstairs, and as soon as I've shown Mr. Warrick to the basement I'll come up and we'll discuss the Gadsden competition."

She shuffled the girls ahead of her, sending them scurrying down to their mothers. Rick stood aside as she walked past him, then followed her down the steps.

"I heard he's been in the penitentiary," a female voice said.

"I wouldn't doubt it," another woman said. "Remember how he was always in trouble?"

"He still looks dangerous, doesn't he?" A third voice asked. "And sinfully handsome."

"Whatever he's been doing these past fifteen years doesn't really matter," Deanie Webber told them. "He's trying to make something of himself now. Ever since he came back to Tuscumbia last summer, he's been a model citizen."

Pausing on the stairway, Lori Lee glanced nervously at the man behind her. Even though he showed no indication she knew he'd heard what was being said about him. She felt the tension emanating from his big body and saw his warm brown eyes turn hard and cold with pain. Instinctively her hand reached out in a comforting gesture, then her common sense took charge and prevented her from actually touching him.

Rick and Lori Lee exchanged an electrically charged stare, the air around them sizzling explosively. Turning around sharply and taking a deep, calming breath, she walked downstairs and opened the door leading to the basement. She flipped on the light switch, revealing the narrow steps.

"It's dark and damp down here," she said. "And a little spooky. There are closed-off tunnels that lead under Main Street."

As they descended the stairs, musty, dank brick walls surrounded them. A single light bulb hanging from the ceiling illuminated the area. Cobwebs dangled from the rafters and spread across the corners like shimmery lace fans.

"You don't have to stay down here with me, Ms. Guy." Rick set his toolbox on top of an old wooden crate. "I'll check things out and see if I can find your problem."

"All right. If you don't need me, I'll go back up to my class."

"I don't need you," he said.

For some reason Lori Lee felt that his words held a double meaning, as if he was warning her away, cautioning her to keep her distance. Did he realize the effect he had on her? Had her interest really been that obvious?

She went back upstairs, hesitating on the top step. She closed her eyes as memories of a long-ago night surged through her. Rick Warrick, a boy with hooded dark eyes and a hungry expression who watched her from a distance, had shown up at a Friday night Debutante Club party after one of Deshler's big games. He wasn't one of their usual crowd and she'd never seen him at one of their parties before, but when she went out on the front porch to look for her boyfriend, Jimmy Davison, she encountered the town bad boy instead. Wearing a brown leather jacket, he leaned against one of the white columns, a beer in his hand and a cigarette in his mouth.

Lori Lee's instincts told her to run, that everything she'd heard about Rick Warrick was true. But her fascination with him, one she shared with almost every other teenage girl in town, overcame her better judgment and she approached him.

"You can't smoke or drink at a Debutante party," Lori Lee told him. "It's against the rules."

"Haven't you heard? I don't follow rules." He tossed the cigarette down on the porch and ground it out with his boot heel.

She was drawn to him, like a flowering plant to the nourishing sun. When she moved close enough to touch him, he set his beer can on the banister rail, grinned devilishly and jerked her into his arms. Her breath caught in her throat. Her eyes widened in surprise and arousal, and her whole body tingled with trembling excitement.

"You don't want to play around with fire, honey. You're liable to get burned."

He kissed her then, his lips covering hers, his tongue forcing her mouth open. She clung to his shoulders, her nails biting into the leather of his jacket. His mouth was hot and wet as it devoured hers. He tasted of smoke and alcohol. When she felt his hand on her buttock, she froze, suddenly aware of what a guy like Rick Warrick would expect from a girl. She was no saint, but she was still a virgin, and she planned on staying one while she was in high school.

Releasing her, he gave her a gentle shove. She staggered backward. "Stay away from me, Lori Lee. I'm bad news for a girl like you."

She'd run from him. Back into the safety of the party. Away from temptation.

Lori Lee opened her eyes, took a deep breath and walked out into the waiting area. Deanie Webber met her before she'd taken ten steps.

"He's still a hunk, isn't he? I mean a drop-dead gorgeous hunk!" Deanie squeezed Lori Lee's arm. "This bunch of biddies in here have been trashing the poor guy, but the truth of the matter is there's not a one who wouldn't love to have him eat crackers in her bed, if you know what I mean."

"Deanie, you'll never change!" Lori Lee smiled at her best friend. "You're as shameless as you were when we were kids."

"He didn't remember me, but I'll bet he remembered you," Deanie said. "I think he always had a thing for you."

Ignoring Deanie's last comment, Lori Lee approached her students and their mothers. "It's too cold in here to get any real practicing done today. I'm afraid we'll have to make it up Friday afternoon."

All the children groaned. The mothers grumbled.

"I know it'll be an inconvenience for all of us, but our next competition is a week from Saturday at Gadsden," Lori Lee reminded them. "I have Twinkle Toes signed up in three categories. Dance-Twirl, Halftime Show Twirl Team and Halftime Show Dance Line."

"You *have* entered Steffie in the solo events we discussed, haven't you?" Mara Royce turned up her tiny pug nose and beamed her hundred-watt phony smile.

"I've entered Steffie in one solo event." Lori Lee often wished that Mara hadn't enrolled her only child in the Dixie Twirlers. The little girl was a spoiled brat, and in Steffie's case, the apple certainly hadn't fallen far from the tree. Mara Royce was a royal pain in the backside. But the woman possessed an enviable position in town. Her father was president of the largest bank in the county and her husband was a highly respected orthodontist.

"I really think Steffie is ready for—" Mara protested.

"Everything is set for the Gadsden competition," Lori Lee said. "Mara, we can discuss this again before we go to Clanton in February."

"We most certainly will discuss it." Mara tilted her sharp chin and pursed her thin lips into a pout.

"Y'all might as well go on home and practice. Hopefully, we'll have some heat by tomorrow." Lori Lee glanced at the partially open door leading to the basement. Once everyone left, she'd be alone in the studio with Rick Warrick. The thought unnerved her and yet excited her.

"Oh, yes," Lori Lee called out as the mothers and daughters bundled up. "Don't forget to stop by next door and pick up your costumes. Aunt Birdie said that they arrived this morning and she's already sorted them and has them ready."

Deanie Webber escorted her six-year-old to the door. "Katie, you go on over and get your costumes. Visit with Miss Birdie a bit. Ask her to give you a cola while you're waiting for me. I'm going to stay and talk to Lori Lee for a few minutes."

Obeying her mother's instructions, Katie rushed outside behind the other girls. Deanie closed the door, blocking out the cold January wind, then turned quickly and hurried back to Lori Lee's side.

"Want me to stick around until he comes up from the basement?" Deanie asked, a coy little grin on her broad face.

"I think I'm perfectly safe with Mr. Warrick." Lori Lee walked over to her desk, opened a bottom drawer and pulled out her beige leather purse.

"I wasn't concerned about your safety. I was worried about whether or not you'd be able to keep your hands off him." Deanie giggled, her cheeks flushed.

Lori Lee unzipped her purse, removed her checkbook and laid it on the desk. "Give it a rest, will you, Deanie? You and Aunt Birdie are the only two people on earth who know about that stupid crush I had on Rick when I was a teenager."

"Do you ever wonder what would have happened if

you'd given in to your basic urges and slept with him?" Deanie flopped down on the lounge area sofa.

"For heaven's sake, I never even had a date with the guy. The only thing that ever happened between us was that one kiss." Lori Lee sat down in the swivel chair behind her desk.

"Yeah, and you've never forgotten that kiss, have you? I'll bet Tory McBain's kisses never turned you on that much."

"I do not want to discuss my ex-husband," Lori Lee said. "And I certainly have no intention of comparing Tory to Rick."

Deanie leaned back on the sofa, burrowing into the cushions until she found a comfortable position. "I've been keeping tabs on him ever since he moved back to town last July."

"And what does Phil think about your taking so much interest in another man?"

Deanie laughed, the sound loud and robust. "My Phil knows he's the only man on earth for me. I've been keeping an eye on Rick for you."

"Well, you've wasted your time." Lori Lee rummaged in her purse, dragging out a pair of beige leather gloves, a pale blue woolen scarf and a gold key chain dripping with an assortment of keys. "When you first told me about Rick being back in town, I made it perfectly clear that I have absolutely no interest in the man."

"I realize you have more men after you than you can handle, but none of them seem to be getting past first base." Deanie eyed the coffeemaker in the makeshift mini-kitchen separated from the rest of the downstairs studio by a pink folding screen. "Fix us some coffee and I'll tell you everything you're dying to know about our Mr. Warrick."

"I do not want to discuss Rick, but I'll fix some coffee. I could use a caffeine boost about now." Lori Lee scooted back her chair, stood and went behind the screen. She filled the coffee machine with water and spooned a chocolate raspberry gourmet blend into the paper filter. "For your information, Powell Goodman and I are seeing quite a lot of each other, and I've dated Jimmy Davison several times since his divorce."

"Two upstanding citizens if there ever were any." Deanie slipped behind the screen, picked up a box of cookies and opened them. "Powell is the biggest stuffed shirt I know, and Jimmy is more in love with himself than he'll ever be with a woman."

"And what is Rick Warrick?" Lori Lee asked. "A sullen, brooding bad boy with no education. A blue-collar worker who lives in his sister's garage apartment."

"Well, well, well. You know a bit more about Rick than you've let on."

"I overhear gossip from time to time."

Deanie dug out a couple of Pecan Sandies from the cookie box. "I hate to tell you this, friend of mine, but you sounded a lot like a snob just then. Aunt Birdie would be appalled that you think you're too good for Rick."

"I don't think I'm... It's just that the last thing I need in my life right now is to get involved with a redneck tough guy. I run a business where I teach young girls. It's important for me to have a good reputation."

"From what I've heard, Rick is working real hard at overcoming his old reputation." Deanie munched on the cookie. "Although rumor has it that he's been seen at the Watering Hole a few times, and he's never been alone."

"I'm sure his taste in women hasn't changed." Reaching on the lower shelf, Lori Lee lifted the sweetener and creamer and placed them beside the coffee machine. "If I remember correctly, he always liked wild girls. The wilder the better."

"Yeah." Deanie sighed. "Wonder what his wife was like? Do you suppose she was a wild woman?"

"I can't imagine Rick married to anyone. He was always too much of a free spirit." Lori Lee poured two cups of coffee, adding sweetener and creamer to both, then handed Deanie a mug decorated with a bright, smiling sun.

"Well, you know his sister, Eve, goes to church with us, and she's been bringing Rick's little girl to every service with her." Deanie sipped her coffee. "She's a gorgeous child. Looks a lot like Rick, except she's fair where he's dark. His wife must have been a blue-eyed blonde."

Rick shoved the basement door wide open. Deanie gasped. Lori Lee's hands trembled.

"Did you find the problem?" Lori Lee asked. She couldn't take her eyes off him. He'd removed his coat, leaving his tight navy sweater to accent every hard line in his upper torso. His faded jeans clung to his hips and cupped him snugly. Lori Lee swallowed.

"Yeah, and it's not good." Rick placed his toolbox on the floor and dropped his coat on top of it. "I'm afraid your unit is a dinosaur. I could make some repairs to keep it going and charge you four or five hundred bucks, but I couldn't guarantee it would last a month."

"I was afraid of that." Lori Lee grimaced, thinking about telling Aunt Birdie that Rick Warrick would be replacing the old heating and cooling system for the studio. Her aunt owned both the building that housed the Dixie Twirlers and Lori Lee's Sparkle and Shine costume shop next door. And her aunt was one of the two people who knew she'd once had a major crush on Rick.

"I can work up an estimate tonight and drop it by sometime tomorrow," Rick said.

"Look, I've got to run." Deanie waved goodbye. "Y'all don't need me. I'll call you later, Lori Lee. Bye now." Deanie kept waving all the way to the front door, then she giggled like an idiot as she slammed the door shut.

"I wish I could remember her," Rick said. "She seems real nice. Are you two friends?"

"Best friends since we were kids. I'm her daughter Katie's godmother."

"She was your best friend in school? The skinny little giggling redhead who was always with you?"

"Then you do remember her. She keeps an auburn rinse on her hair now and she's put on a few pounds, but she's still the same giggling girl. She married Phil Webber. He was senior class president the year I graduated."

"She told me her daughter is one of your students." Rick shoved his hands into the front pockets of his jeans. "Are you taking any new students right now? I mean, I know it's in the middle of the year and all."

"I take new students all the time," Lori Lee told him. "I have classes for ages three to fourteen, and I give private lessons to older girls and to students who excel, or those who need a little extra help."

Rick glanced at the hot-pink mug she held in her hand. "Don't let me keep you from drinking your coffee. It'll get cold."

"Oh." She had forgotten all about the mug until he reminded her. "Would you care for some coffee? I just made a fresh pot."

"It'd be too much trouble."

"Don't be silly. Sit down. I'll get you some."

Why had she invited him to stay? Why was she pouring him a cup of coffee? Had she lost her mind? A guy like this wouldn't need much encouragement before he moved in and took over. She'd had sense enough at seventeen to steer clear of him. Why wasn't she that smart now?

"How do you take your coffee, Mr. Warrick?"

"Black. And call me Rick."

She handed him a mug, being careful not to touch him. "Please do sit down."

When he sat on the sofa, she perched on the edge of the chair across from him. As they sipped their coffee, they stole quick glances at each other.

"How much do you charge for lessons?" he asked.

"I charge by the month. Two classes a week. The basic

fee is thirty-five dollars, but that doesn't include extras like costumes and—''

"I'd like to enroll my daughter." He took several gulps of the hot black liquid, then placed his mug on the metal-and-glass coffee table in front of him. "She's six, in the first grade at Southside. I'd like for her to make friends with the kind of little girls I saw here today."

"Has she ever taken dance or baton lessons before?"

"Nope. But I bought her a baton for Christmas a couple of years ago and she plays with it all the time."

"She would have to start out in the beginners' class with our three-to-six-year-olds. When she begins to show progress, I'll move her up into Twinkle Toes."

"She's sort of shy, and I'm afraid she'll turn out to be a loner like her old man. I don't want that," Rick said. "I'd like for her to fit in and be accepted."

The way I never was. He didn't say the words, but Lori Lee knew what he meant. She hadn't known much about Rick, except that he'd been shuffled from one foster home to another, and that his younger sister, Eve, had been adopted by a good family who hadn't wanted Rick. No one had wanted the hellion he'd been back then.

"What's your daughter's name?"

"Darcie."

"Well, bring Darcie by the studio tomorrow afternoon so she can meet the other girls in the beginners' class, and we'll show her what twirling is all about."

"I don't know if I can take time off from work tomorrow, but I'll see what I can manage. If I can't bring her, I'll get my sister to."

"You're going to drop by with the estimate for the new heat and air system by tomorrow, aren't you?" Lori Lee asked.

"Yeah."

"Bring the estimate by at the same time you bring Darcie, that way you won't be taking time away from your job," Lori Lee suggested. "Since my Aunt Birdie owns the building, I'll have her come over and talk to you while I show Darcie around the studio and introduce her to the other girls.''

"Yeah. Sure. Thanks.'' Rick stood, walked over and picked up his coat. He slipped into it and lifted his toolbox. "See you tomorrow.''

"Yes, see you tomorrow. You and Darcie.''

She followed him, pausing when he opened the front door and turned to face her. "Look, Lori Lee, I know when I left this town, people were glad to see me go. I'd earned myself a pretty bad reputation.''

"That was a long time ago.'' She could smell his sweat, not an offensive odor, just a rough, masculine scent that blended with the clean smell of his clothes and hair.

"I haven't been a saint these past fifteen years, but I'm doing my best to settle down and provide a home for my daughter.'' He stared into Lori Lee's big blue eyes and felt himself drowning. If he'd known she had moved back to Tuscumbia, would he have come home? "Darcie is my main concern. Everything I do, I do for her.''

"I understand,'' Lori Lee said.

He nodded, then turned and walked out the door and down the sidewalk to his parked minivan, Bobo Lewis Heating And Air-Conditioning printed on the side in bold black lettering. She stood in the doorway and watched him until he drove down Main Street and the van disappeared around the corner on Fifth.

She'd told him she understood his devotion to his child, and she did. If she had a little girl, she would make her daughter the center of her universe. But she could never have the one thing she wanted most—a child of her own. Regret knotted her stomach. Sorrow clogged her throat with unshed tears.

Lori Lee went back inside the studio, sat on the edge of her desk and flipped through her Rolodex, then made her first telephone call to cancel her private lessons for the day.

* * *

Lori Lee chopped up the pack of lunch meat into tiny pieces and dumped it into Tyke's doggie bowl. The brindled Boston terrier jumped up and down, gazing at Lori Lee with huge brown eyes.

She set the bowl on the floor and petted Tyke on the head. "Here you go, baby. Eat up while I fix my supper."

While Tyke gobbled up his meal, Lori Lee removed a single-serving casserole from the refrigerator and popped it into the microwave. As she waited for her dinner to warm, she poured herself a cup of coffee and sat down at the round table that was dressed in lace and floral fabric matching the kitchen wallpaper.

Leaning back in the cane-bottom oak chair, she sighed. It had been a long day. She was tired, hungry and unnerved. She'd decided to wait until morning to tell Aunt Birdie the bad news about the central heat and air at the studio. She wasn't overly concerned about the expense for her aunt, who probably had enough money to buy and sell the whole town. Birdie's fifth husband had left her millions, and she'd been far from poor before Hubert Pierpont's death. No, what Lori Lee dreaded was telling her aunt that Rick Warrick would be installing the new heating equipment and that he planned to enroll his daughter in the twirlers.

Birdie Guy Jackson Lovvorn Hill McWilliams Pierpont was a woman who loved men and simply couldn't understand how her favorite niece had gone nearly six years without a significant other. As far as Aunt Birdie was concerned, dating didn't count. A woman needed to be in love, and if she were in love, she should either be living with the object of her affection or married to him. Lori Lee fell short on all counts.

Aunt Birdie had been Lori Lee's confidante as long as she could remember. She'd told her aunt things she'd never even told Deanie. And since her parents had moved to Naples, Florida, three years ago, after her younger brother Ronnie's death, Lori Lee had become even closer to Birdie. Maybe it was her aunt's big, warm heart or her zest for life that had always assured Lori Lee that Birdie would not only understand but sympathize.

If she had listened to her crazy Aunt Birdie's advice when she was seventeen, Lori Lee would have acted on her feelings for Rick Warrick and ridden off with him on his motorcycle in the middle of the night. But Rick had frightened her, and she'd kept her distance, seldom even speaking to him. But in her dreams, awake or asleep, she had fantasized about being his woman.

She wasn't a teenage girl anymore. She was an adult who had just turned thirty-two on her last birthday. She was old enough to know better than to allow her hormones to dictate her actions. And her hormones had certainly gone into overdrive this afternoon when Rick Warrick reentered her world.

It wasn't as if there weren't men in her life. Actually there were more men chasing her than she knew what to do with, but not one of them made her stomach do flip-flops or her blood sizzle with excitement. Ever since her divorce from Tory had become final and she'd moved back to Tuscumbia, there had been a steady stream of eligible, and a few not so eligible, men beating a path to her door. Several of those men had offered her marriage, but she had declined.

She'd been madly in love with Tory McBain, the big, handsome star quarterback for the University of Alabama, whom she'd married at twenty-two and divorced four years later. Their marriage had ended badly, leaving both her heart and spirit broken. But Lori Lee knew one thing for certain, she would never marry again until she could love someone else with that same kind of wondrous passion.

She supposed what upset her the most about being exposed to Rick's rough and rugged brand of male sensuality was that she was still as scared of him as she'd ever been. The effect he had on her frightened her because it was stronger than anything she'd ever felt. Not even her love for Tory had been as powerful.

But she didn't love Rick. How could she? She barely knew him. No, she didn't love the man. She just wanted him—wanted him in a desperate, almost savage way she had never wanted anyone else.

Two

Rick set two bowls of vegetable soup beside the plastic spoons and paper napkins on the card table. He wasn't much of a cook, but he made sure Darcie got three decent meals a day. A couple of times a week, they ate supper at his sister's, but he tried not to impose on Eve more than he had to. She already did too much for them, and Rick accepted her help only for Darcie's sake. In the two years since his ex-wife's death, he had discovered just how difficult it was for a single man to raise a child alone. Especially a tiny, shy, insecure little girl who was just now beginning to trust him enough to believe he wouldn't leave her.

When April had been killed in a car crash, along with her drunken boyfriend, Rick had had no choice but to take Darcie on the road with him. He'd been a construction worker most of his adult life, ever since he'd done his stint in the army. Seven years ago, he had wound up in Mercy Falls, South Dakota, where he'd met a barfly named April

Denton. April had been a looker. Big blue eyes. Long blond hair. And a body to die for. The first time he saw her, he'd thought of Lori Lee Guy. There'd been a striking resemblance between the two, but where Lori Lee was a class act—a Southern belle with a pedigree as long as his arm—April had been cheap and flashy. They'd burned themselves out after a few weeks of passion, and Rick had moved on to another town and another woman. Then April had called him and told him she was pregnant. He hadn't wanted to marry her, but in the end he had. He'd done it for the child, even though he hadn't been sure, at the time, the baby was really his. No kid deserved to come into this world unloved and unwanted, as he'd been.

"Daddy, are the grilled cheese sandwiches ready?" Darcie asked.

"Huh?" Rick's mind jumped from the past to the present. He picked up the metal spatula and flipped the sandwiches in the electric skillet. "Any minute now, sweetie. Go ahead and start on your soup if you're hungry."

"Shouldn't I say grace first? They always say it at Aunt Eve's before they eat."

"Sure. Say grace." Rick bowed his head.

"God is great, God is good. Now let us thank him for our food. Amen." Darcie looked up at her father and smiled.

Her two front teeth were missing. He hadn't known a damn thing about the tooth fairy until Eve had explained all about the mysterious spirit who gathered up teeth from beneath children's pillows and left money in their place. Darcie's two front teeth had cost Rick four bucks—two dollars a tooth. Eve had told him that front teeth were more expensive, and in the future a dollar a tooth would suffice.

Rick lifted a sandwich and placed it on a paper plate beside Darcie's soup bowl, then repeated the procedure with his sandwich. He pulled out a folding chair and sat down across from his daughter.

"Am I going to have to stay over at Aunt Eve's tonight?'' Darcie slurped her soup, then took a bite out of her sandwich.

"I'm afraid so. I've got to work, and you're just not old enough to stay out here in the apartment by yourself.''

Rick hated leaving Darcie alone several nights a week, but he had no choice. If he wanted to earn enough money to buy Bobo's half of the business before the old man retired, he had to work a second job, if only part-time. His and Darcie's future depended on him, on his making a place for them in the community and earning enough money to give Darcie the kind of life he'd never had.

He wanted his daughter to have every opportunity, and it was up to him to make sure she got the chances she deserved. If only the right people would accept her, allow her to become friends with their children and invite her into their inner circle, Rick would pay any price. But with his former reputation and past history hanging around his neck like an albatross, finding acceptance for himself and his daughter in Tuscumbia might prove an impossible task. But he sure as hell was trying. If they'd just give him a chance, he'd show the good citizens how much he had changed, how determined he was to be a good person, too. He'd do just about anything for Darcie's sake.

"What kind of car is it you're fixing for that man?'' Darcie asked.

"It's a 1959 Corvette,'' Rick said. "And the man I'm restoring the car for is Powell Goodman. He's a lawyer and a pretty important guy around these parts. His father and grandfather were both judges.''

"Aren't you an important man, Daddy?''

Important? Him? To most people he was about as important as yesterday's trash. "I'm just an ordinary guy, sweetie. A man trying to make ends meet and give his kid a better life than he had.''

Darcie scooted out of her chair, walked around the table and, standing on tiptoe, flung her arms around her father's neck. "You're an important man to me, Daddy. Very, very important."

If Rick had been an emotional man, he might have teared up at his child's sweet, loving proclamation. But Rick hadn't shed a tear since he'd been younger than Darcie was now. He'd learned early on that nobody gave a tinker's damn whether he was upset, lonely or hurt. Poor little A.K. Had his own parents ever loved him? Sometimes he wondered if his mother had given him only initials for a first name because it had been quick and easy, no bother for her. But by the time he was in junior high, all his buddies called him Rick, taken from Warrick. And to this day, he preferred the nickname over the solitary initials on his birth certificate.

Rick hugged his daughter, kissed her on her forehead and nuzzled her nose with his. She giggled gleefully. "Thanks, big girl. I think you're a pretty important person, too."

"Snooky-nose me again, Daddy." Darcie pressed her tiny button nose against her father's long, lean, hawkish nose.

She loved to play what Rick had dubbed "snooky-nose," where they rubbed their noses together. He repeated the nuzzling, then lifted her and set her down in her chair. "Eat your supper, young lady. I've got fifteen minutes to eat, clean up our mess and get you over to Aunt Eve's."

"When you own all of Mr. Bobo's business, then will you be able to stay home with me every night?" Darcie lifted her grilled cheese sandwich.

"You bet." Rick devoured his soup and sandwich, occasionally glancing at his daughter who nibbled at her food.

He supposed he should see April every time he looked at Darcie. She had the same blond hair and blue eyes, but since she'd been a toddler, every time he looked at his daughter he saw himself—and Lori Lee. Darcie had his facial structure, his wide mouth with a thick bottom lip and his prominent chin, but she was all blond, blue-eyed loveliness like Lori Lee. Once he'd realized Darcie really was his child, he had fantasized that Lori Lee was her mother instead of April.

More than anything, he wanted his daughter to become the kind of woman Lori Lee Guy was.

"While I clean up here, you get your pajamas and your school clothes for tomorrow ready to take over to Aunt Eve's."

"Okay, Daddy."

He knew he had to bring up the subject of enrolling her in the Dixie Twirlers, but he wasn't quite sure how she'd react. Darcie was shy and had had a difficult time making friends at school.

"Hey, Darcie, how would you like to take baton lessons from a very nice lady?" Rick dumped their disposable utensils, bowls, plates and cups into the garbage sack.

"Do you mean Miss Lori Lee's twirlers, Daddy?" Darcie clutched her footed pajamas to her chest. "The Dixie Twirlers?"

"You've already heard about them, I see."

"Oh, yes, Daddy. Steffie Royce and Katie Webber are in Twinkle Toes. They get to go to contests and march in parades and—"

"Do I take this enthusiasm to mean you'd like to enroll in classes?" Rick scoured the soup pot with steel wool, then rinsed the container and turned it upside down on the drainboard.

"Can I really? You aren't kidding me, are you?"

"Tomorrow, after school, Aunt Eve can bring you by the shop, and when I take over an estimate to Miss Lori Lee on a new heating and cooling system, you can go with me. I told her about you today. She wants you to meet the other girls in her beginners' class and see if you want to join them."

"I want to join them. I want to join them!" Darcie jumped up and down, then flew across the room and into her father's arms. "You're the best daddy in the whole wide world!"

Dear God, what had he ever done to deserve this precious child? He knew he was far from the best father in the world, but if love and devotion counted for anything, then maybe he had a chance of someday earning that title.

"Well, well," Birdie Pierpont mused, dramatically rolling her big green eyes heavenward. "Life never ceases to amaze me. Just when I'd given up hope of you ever awakening from your hundred-year celibate sleep, along comes Prince Charming to awaken you with a sweet kiss."

"Rick Warrick is no Prince Charming," Lori Lee said. "And he's certainly not going to awaken me with a kiss."

"No, you're quite right, sugar. Rick is more a beast than a prince, and I imagine his kisses are more passionate than sweet."

"Argh!" Lori Lee stormed out from behind the checkout counter in her costume shop and straightened a perfectly straight row of leotards folded neatly on a table. "This is the very reason I didn't want to even mention Rick's name to you. I knew you'd start cooking up some scheme in that evil brain of yours."

"Thank you, sugar, for the compliment. So seldom does anyone appreciate a truly evil brain these days." Birdie, all two hundred pounds, five feet four inches of her, rounded the corner of the counter and followed her niece.

"I wish I'd never told you about my crush on Rick when I was a teenager. Mother would have been shocked senseless if I'd ever told her that you advised me to go riding off on his motorcycle with him."

"Look, my dear Miss Prim and Proper." Birdie planted her pudgy hands on her wide hips. "You've been as fidgety as a worm in hot ashes ever since you learned that A. K. Warrick was back in Tuscumbia." When Lori Lee opened her mouth to protest, her aunt held up a restraining hand. "No, no. Don't you dare deny it. Since your divorce, you've led all the men around here on a merry chase, but not once have I seen you foaming at the mouth. Not until now."

"Birdie Lou Pierpont, you have the most vulgar way of expressing yourself." Lori Lee leaned over into the front window, got on her knees and began fiddling with the display. "I am not foaming at the mouth."

"I've been accused of worse things than vulgarity." Birdie fluffed her curly white-blond hair. "It wouldn't hurt you to come down off that pedestal the men in town have placed you on and get a little vulgar yourself. I'll bet Rick could teach you how to get down and dirty."

Lori Lee crawled out of the display window, turned sharply and glared at her aunt. "Will you please stop this? Rick is going to be here any minute to bring us the estimate for the new heat and air system, and he's bringing his daughter with him. I want you to promise me that you'll be on your best behavior."

Puckering her mouth into a sulk, Birdie crossed her fat arms over her ample bosom and let out a loud huff.

Lori Lee loved her Aunt Birdie dearly, but more often than not the woman tried her patience. She'd never been able to understand how her straitlaced, churchgoing, engineer father could possibly have an older sister as wild, zany and totally unorthodox as Birdie.

"I've seen him and his little girl, you know." Birdie inspected her clawlike red fingernails.

"Where?"

"Around."

"You never mentioned it to me."

"I knew you'd been trying to avoid him," Birdie said. "But I also knew that in a town this size, your paths were bound to cross sooner or later."

"I have not been avoiding him! There is nothing going on between Rick and me. There never has been. There never will be. He's going to oversee the installation of the new heat and air system, and I'll see him when he drops his daughter by for classes and picks her up. That's the beginning and end of my association with Mr. A. K. Warrick."

"Fine. Far be it from me to interfere in your dull, lonely life."

"My life is neither dull nor lonely, thank you very much."

"Oh, don't thank me, my dear." Birdie smiled, cracking her full face into dozens of tiny, thin wrinkles. "You must thank men like Powell Goodman and Jimmy Davison for filling your life with so much passion and excitement."

"I'm not looking for passion and excitement!"

"Pity." Birdie tsk-tsked and shook her head sadly. "Rick would be just the man to give you both, but since you're not interested... Of course, he does have one thing you might want."

"There's nothing he has that I want."

"Are you sure?"

"I'm sure," Lori Lee said adamantly.

"Not even his child?"

"Are you implying that... For your information, several of the men I date have children, *if* I wanted a man for that reason."

"Yes, but all of the ones with children also have ex-wives," Birdie reminded her. "I understand Rick's wife is dead."

"I'm going to say this one more time, and then we're not ever going to have this discussion again. Rick is not my type. He wasn't fifteen years ago, and he's not now. We have nothing in common."

The front door opened and the UPS carrier delivered a large box. Lori Lee signed for the package, exchanged pleasantries with the deliveryman and lifted the box to the top of the checkout counter.

Just as she found a knife and positioned it to rip apart the box, the door opened again. She glanced up and her heartbeat accelerated. Rick walked in holding the hand of the little, blond angel at his side. Lori Lee glanced back and forth from Rick to his child. Tears misted her eyes. She looked down, concentrating on opening the box, trying desperately to hide her reaction.

Rick's little girl could be her little girl. The little girl Lori Lee had carried in her body for five months. The little girl who'd been unable to live outside her mother's body.

"Well, Rick, how are you?" Birdie padded across the floor in her sock feet, leaned down and held out her hand. "Hello there, cutie. You must be Darcie Warrick."

"How'd you know my name?" the child asked, gazing up at Birdie, a tenuous smile quivering on her lips.

"Aunt Birdie knows all sorts of things about people," Birdie said. "Especially people who interest me. And you, Darcie, interest me a great deal."

"I do?"

"Yes, you do."

"Why?"

"Well, you come with me and I'll get you a cola and show you all the wondrous things in our little Sparkle and Shine shop here, then I'll tell you why you interest me so." Birdie offered Darcie her hand. The child accepted, then looked to her father for approval.

"It's fine, sweetie. You go with Miss Birdie," Rick said.

"And you—" Birdie pointed to Rick "—take my niece over to the studio and discuss business. When you two come to a decision, I'll sign whatever papers are necessary and write out a check."

When Rick and Lori Lee didn't respond, just glanced awkwardly at each other, Birdie shooed them with a wave of her hand. "Go on, now. Darcie and I will be over to the studio by the time the beginners' class starts."

"We can discuss things here, if you prefer," Rick told Lori Lee, sensing her reluctance to go to the studio alone with him.

"No, we'll leave and pacify Aunt Birdie. She loves to fill children's heads with all kinds of nonsensical stories while she gives them a grand tour. And kids usually love looking at all our costumes and supplies.''

"I'll bet y'all do a booming business around Halloween." Rick surveyed the shop, noticing the wide variety of items, everything from ballet slippers and majorette boots to magic wands and drum major batons.

"We do a good business year-round," Lori Lee told him. "We supply all our twirlers, the Deshler band and majorettes and several of the dance studios, as well as a little theater group."

"Sounds like you're doing all right." Rick wondered just how much Lori Lee depended on her two jobs for an income. She'd been born into an upper middle class family, and he'd heard that not only had she inherited money from her maternal grandparents, but that her aunt was filthy rich.

"I make a good living," Lori Lee said. "Come on. While you explain what I need to know about your installing the new heat and air system, I'll show you around my studio and give you an idea of what all is involved in your daughter—in Darcie—taking lessons."

Rick followed Lori Lee out of the Sparkle and Shine shop to the studio in the adjacent building. He watched the way she walked, a seductive hip-swaying come-on that she wasn't even aware of. He'd known a lot of women in his thirty-three years, but he'd never known anyone as beautiful as Lori Lee Guy. How the hell had a woman like her remained single so long after her divorce? Had her ex-husband done such a number on her that he had scared her off marriage forever?

"Come on in," she said, unlocking the door.

The moment he stepped inside, Rick felt the warmth. Puzzled at first, he surveyed the studio and discovered that she'd strategically placed small electric heaters around the room.

"I'm going to hold classes down here until the new heating system is put it," she said. "I've closed off the upstairs temporarily. I simply can't postpone any more classes. We're going to Gadsden next weekend for a competition.''

Rick reached inside his jacket and pulled out the estimate. He'd worked it up around midnight last night, after he returned from the garage he rented on a monthly basis so he'd have a place to restore Powell Goodman's 'Vette.

"Here's the estimate. The price covers everything." He handed her the papers. "Look it over and let me know if you have any questions."

"Let's sit down." She nodded toward the lounge area. "Would you like some coffee? I can put some on."

"Don't go to any trouble for me."

"No, no trouble. I usually have a pot waiting for the mothers who like to stay and chat while their daughters are in class."

She glanced over the estimate quickly, noting every detail and deciding immediately that the cost seemed reasonable.

"I noticed that several of Tuscumbia's best families have their daughters in your classes." Rick stuffed his hands in his pockets, then lifted his heels off the floor repeatedly as he craned his neck backward and glanced around the studio. "I want Darcie to be accepted." He cleared his throat. "I don't want who I am or who I was to... Well, you know what I'm trying to say. I never fit in. I was always an outsider. I don't want that for my little girl."

The way he said *my little girl* hit a sympathetic cord inside Lori Lee. No matter what his sins were—past and present—it was obvious that Rick loved his daughter.

"I can't promise you that having Darcie enrolled here at Dixie Twirlers will ensure her popularity, but...well, I'll certainly do what I can to see that she fits in and feels a part of everything we do." Lori Lee tossed the estimate on the sofa, then busied herself preparing the coffee machine.

"She's all excited about taking lessons," Rick said. "She's a little shy and I was afraid she might feel uncomfortable around a group of kids she doesn't know, but she's been jumping for joy ever since I mentioned it to her."

"I'll start her out in the beginners' class," Lori Lee explained. "She'll need two batons. One for class and one for competition. We sell them next door at Sparkle and Shine."

Rick grinned, his sexy, captivating smile that turned Lori Lee's stomach inside out. Why couldn't Powell's smile do that to her? Or Jimmy's? Why was it that no one had ever affected her the way Rick did?

"You tell me what she needs and I'll be sure she has it." Rick couldn't afford the lessons, let alone anything extra. Every dime he made, that he didn't spend on Darcie, went into savings. That's why he didn't have any decent clothes, still wore a fifteen-year-old leather jacket and worn-out boots and went months between haircuts.

"I think Darcie's a lucky little girl to have a father like you." Lori Lee kept her back to Rick as she removed two mugs from the wall rack. "And the strange thing about it is that I never pictured you as a father. You were always too wild and free."

"Darcie wasn't planned," Rick admitted. "She was an accident. I got April pregnant, so I married her for the kid's sake. We stayed married less than a year." Rick slumped down in a cushioned Windsor chair to the left of the sofa. "Believe me, Lori Lee, my daughter isn't so lucky. April was a lousy mother and I was an absentee father who saw Darcie about once a month. I sent support checks, but April blew them on liquor and good times for herself."

"You don't have to tell me any of this. It's none of my business." Lori Lee wasn't sure she wanted to share confidences with Rick. Doing so made their relationship more personal, and that was the last thing she wanted.

"If you're going to help Darcie, you need to know that until we moved to Tuscumbia last summer she hadn't had much of a life."

"What happened to your wife? Your ex-wife?" Lori Lee

poured coffee into two mugs, seasoned hers to taste and
lifted the mugs off the table.

"April was killed in a car wreck two years ago." Rick
accepted the coffee when Lori Lee offered it to him. Her
hand grazed his. He looked up into her startled blue eyes
and realized that on some level she was afraid of him.

He set his mug down on the coffee table, and when Lori
Lee sat down across from him, he reached out to touch her
reassuringly. Grasping her mug with both hands, she
scooted back on the sofa.

"I decided to bring Darcie home to Tuscumbia because
I knew it would be the only way she'd ever have a normal
life." Rick lifted the mug off the table and to his lips. He
took several sips. "I used my life savings to buy half-
ownership in Bobo Lewis's business, and I'm hoping to
buy him out when he retires. I'm trying to be an upstanding
citizen, for Darcie's sake. And one of these days, I'd like
to find a nice woman, get married and give Darcie a real
mother and a bunch of brothers and sisters."

I don't care, Lori Lee wanted to scream. *I do not care!*
Why should it matter to me that Rick Warrick wants a
houseful of kids? He doesn't mean a thing to me. His
dreams aren't important to me.

"Is something wrong?" he asked. "You're awfully
quiet, and you've got a strange look on your face."

"No, nothing's wrong. I'm fine," she lied. "I think you
have some very worthwhile plans and I wish you the very
best luck in…well, in buying out Bobo and in finding Darcie a new mother."

"Yeah, thanks," Rick said. "My sister Eve's been set-
ting up some dates for me, but nothing's panned out yet.
And I got a few dates on my own, but unfortunately they
weren't good mother material, if you know what I mean?"

Rick chuckled like a naughty little boy, and something
inside Lori Lee wanted to slap his face. He was such a
chauvinist, but then, he always had been. She supposed one
of his many fascinations for the female sex was his blatant

unrepentant macho attitude. Why was it that women were intrigued by bad boys? Even she harbored a secret fantasy that she was the only woman on earth capable of taming Rick Warrick, of turning her own bad boy into a model husband and father.

But Rick wanted more children.

Lori Lee tried to smile, but the effort failed miserably. Instead she sipped her coffee, picked up the estimate folder and pretended to thoroughly inspect every page.

Rick knew he'd put his foot in his mouth when he'd mentioned "those kind of women." He supposed he'd always considered bad girls the only kind of girls a bad boy like him deserved. He had to admit that bad girls were a lot more fun if all a guy wanted was a good time.

He'd tried to work up some enthusiasm over the women Eve found for him to date, but not even a hungry good-night kiss had gotten his motor running. Maybe nice girls just didn't turn him on.

No, that wasn't exactly true. There was one nice girl who'd always given him a hard-on just looking at her, and she still did. Rick squirmed uncomfortably in the chair. What the hell was he supposed to do now? He was sitting there, getting harder every minute, in a studio that would soon be filled with a bunch of tiny tots, one of which was his own daughter.

He had to get his mind off his favorite fantasy—making love to Lori Lee. He knew he wasn't good enough for her, that she'd never even date him let alone consider marrying him. But since his return to Tuscumbia, he had found himself daydreaming about making love to Lori Lee, then making her his wife and the mother of his child.

If he shared that particular fantasy with her, she'd probably laugh in his face and ask him just who he thought he was. What would she want with a guy like him when she could have her pick of successful, respectable men? Men like Jimmy Davison and Powell Goodman. How could he ever compete with men who could offer her everything?

The silence between them stretched into hour-long minutes. Lori Lee glanced at the wall clock. Any second now her students for the five-thirty class would come barreling through the front door.

"I, uh, I have to get ready for my class." She stood, then handed him the estimate. "Everything looks fine to me. Show this to Aunt Birdie and she'll write you a check. When can you start on the job?"

"We're booked up until next Monday." Standing, he shoved his hands in his jacket pockets and dragged the jacket down over the front of his jeans. "I'll get my crew out here first thing Monday morning. About eight o'clock, if somebody can be here to let us in."

"That'll be fine. I'll meet you here." This was Thursday. She wouldn't see him again until Monday. That gave her the entire weekend to get her hormones under control so she didn't make a fool of herself around Rick. She had to keep reminding herself that he'd been bad news fifteen years ago, and he still was.

Darcie came flying threw the open door, Birdie waddling feistily behind her.

Jumping up and down beside her father, Darcie held up a shiny new baton. "Look what Aunt Birdie gave me. It's my very own superstar baton."

Willing his body to relax, Rick grinned and nodded his head. "Yeah, that's some great-looking baton." He glanced over at Birdie. "I'll pay you for it, of course."

"Nonsense," Birdie said. "This was a gift for my new little friend. You can buy her the classic baton for competition."

"Thanks, Miss Birdie." Rick wondered if Birdie Pierpont had any idea how hard-pressed for cash he was and had taken pity on him. He hoped not. The one thing he hated most was pity.

"The other girls will be here shortly, Darcie," Lori Lee said. "Would you like for me to give you your first lesson before they get here?"

"Oh, yes, Miss Lori Lee." Gripping her baton tightly, Darcie stood at attention in front of her teacher. "What do I do first?"

"Come with me." Lori Lee placed her hand on the child's shoulder and led her to the center of the room. "Tell me, Darcie, do you know how to dip ice cream?"

"What?"

"Can you dip ice cream?" Lori Lee repeated. "You know, with an ice cream scoop."

"Yes, I know how to do that. Why?"

"Because that's what I want you to do with your baton."

Darcie looked at Lori Lee, puzzlement in her stare. "You want me to dip ice cream with my baton?"

Lori Lee reached over and removed one of her batons from the wall rack where she displayed them. Gripping the wand in the middle, she delved it downward to the left, then lifted it and delved downward to the right.

"See what I did? I'm pretending my baton is a double ice cream scoop. On this side—" she dipped to the left "—is chocolate ice cream, and on this side—" she dipped to the right "—is vanilla ice cream."

Darcie smiled and nodded her head. "I get it." Watching again while Lori Lee demonstrated, Darcie scooped to the left, then to the right. "Look, Daddy, I'm scooping ice cream with my baton."

"And doing a great job, sweetie." His eyes met Lori Lee's and for just an instant they shared the joy of Darcie's triumphant happiness. "She catches on quick, doesn't she, Miss Lori Lee?" Rick asked.

"She's a natural. She'll be moving up to Twinkle Toes in no time." Lori Lee focused all her attention on Darcie. "Now, let me show you another exercise."

Rick watched his daughter for several more minutes, then turned to Birdie and held out the estimate. "Lori Lee has okayed this, and I told her we can start work Monday morning. I won't need any payment until the job's done. It shouldn't take more than one day, two at the most."

Birdie waved the estimate away. "I don't need to see the thing. Just put in whatever this old building needs to make it warm in the winter and cool in the summer."

"I think we can manage that."

"How much extra would you charge to make the job last an extra day or two?" Birdie cocked her head to one side, avoiding eye contact with Rick.

"Why would you want the project to—"

"To give you and Lori Lee a little more time together," Birdie freely admitted. "It doesn't look like y'all can think up any excuses on your own for seeing each other, so I thought I'd help out. After all, you've been in town five months and neither you nor Lori Lee had made a move to contact each other."

"Miss Birdie, what are you saying? I can assure you that there's nothing going on between your niece and me."

"Yes, I'm well aware that there isn't. I just want to know why not." Easing up beside Rick, Birdie slipped her fleshy arm around his waist. "You're single. Lori Lee's single. And it's obvious to me that y'all have got the hots for each other."

"You're a plainspoken woman, aren't you, Miss Birdie."

"Call me Aunt Birdie." She hugged him around the waist.

"Well, Aunt Birdie, tell me why you'd want your niece involved with a man like me? You know my reputation. I'm a bad boy from the wrong side of the tracks. I barely got out of high school and I've worked construction most of my life. What do I have to offer a woman like Lori Lee?"

"She's been afraid to fall in love again since her divorce," Birdie told him. "She's bombarded by the attention of all these lackluster Romeos. What she needs is a real man for a change. Somebody who'll stir her blood." Birdie jabbed him in the center of his chest with her index finger. "That's you. A woman would have to be dead for you not to stir her blood."

Rick grinned. Damn, but he liked Lori Lee's Aunt Birdie. She was his kind of woman. "Even if Lori Lee was interested in me, which she's not, what makes you think I'd be interested in her?"

The front door burst open and three little girls came rushing in, one breathless mother following them. Lori Lee gathered them together and introduced them to Darcie.

"Your daughter is a lovely child," Aunt Birdie told Rick.

"Yes, she is, but my daughter's looks have nothing to do with the question I asked you."

"I think maybe it does." Birdie told him, then smiled at the harried young mother who approached them. "Hello, Mindy. How are you today?"

"Running around in circles as usual," Mindy said. "Who's this? A new twirler father?"

"Forgive my lack of manners." Birdie patted Rick on the arm. "Mindy, this is Rick Warrick, Darcie's father." Birdie nodded toward the newcomer. "Rick, this is Mindy Jenkins. She's the mother of the little brunette over there, and aunt to the redheaded twins."

"Well, welcome to the twirling world," Mindy said. "Just be prepared for your little girl to sleep, eat and bathe with her baton for the next few months."

"Don't you think Rick's daughter is a living doll?" Birdie asked. "I was just about to tell Rick how much she reminds me of Lori Lee at that age. Do you see the resemblance, Mindy?"

Mindy stared at Darcie, then at Lori Lee. She smacked her lips. "Glory be, you're right. I swear, they look enough alike to be mother and daughter."

"Your wife must have been a very pretty blonde," Birdie said. "I imagine she looked a lot like Lori Lee."

Damn smart old woman, Rick thought. Was she psychic or something? Without actually accusing him of choosing a woman who had reminded him of Lori Lee, Birdie let Rick know she'd figured out just why he'd been attracted to his former wife.

"Yeah, she looked a bit like Lori Lee, but that's where any similarity between the two ended."

Rick had to admit that he had a weakness for blondes, especially blue-eyed blondes with pouty lips and hourglass figures. He supposed he'd looked for Lori Lee in every woman he'd been with since he'd left Tuscumbia fifteen years ago. He'd been with plenty of cheap imitations, Darcie's mother being the closest thing he'd found to his fantasy woman. At least in the looks department. It hadn't taken Rick long to discover April Denton was no lady. But then, it hadn't mattered. He sure as hell had never been a gentleman.

Since the day he realized Darcie was really his, he'd thought back to when she'd been conceived, wondering why he'd been fool enough to have sex with a woman without using protection. He wasn't usually that careless.

He could recall only one night that it could have happened. The first night he'd had sex with April. The night he'd taken April Denton to bed and made love to Lori Lee Guy.

Three

It was a slow day at the Sparkle and Shine shop, slower than usual for a Monday in January. A cold drizzle had set in a little after eleven, and Lori Lee could tell by the clinking taps on the awnings that the rain was mixed with sleet. She hoped the weather didn't worsen and force her to cancel the afternoon and evening classes. All the competition groups needed this last week of practice before they performed in Gadsden on Saturday.

"Where are those tights with the pink and red hearts on them?" Aunt Birdie called from the storage room. "I wanted to plan our Valentine display for the window. I've got to find something to keep me busy. It doesn't look like we're going to have any customers."

"Mondays are always slow," Lori Lee said. "Besides, the weather's getting nasty. And we sold out of those tights last year. I have some ordered and expect them in any day now."

"Well, I can't find anything else to get into back here."

Emerging from the storage room, Birdie pulled a pack of cards out of her yellow smock pocket. "We could play a few games to pass the time."

"You don't want to play cards," Lori Lee said. "You want to talk, to ask me a dozen questions about my date Saturday night."

"I couldn't care less about your Saturday night with Powell." Birdie slipped the cards back in her pocket. "Even if you slept with him, I'd probably find the retelling as boring as you found the actual event."

Lori Lee tried not to laugh, but several muffled giggles escaped. "I didn't sleep with Powell."

"I didn't think you did."

"We went to a play at the Ritz and had a late dinner at the Renaissance Tower."

"That's nice, dear." Birdie walked over to the front door and looked outside. "It's just a coming down, isn't it? Good thing Rick and his crew are working inside."

"I wondered how long it would take you to get around to talking about Rick." Lori Lee walked over and placed her arm around her aunt's shoulders. "I saw him this morning at the studio for all of about five minutes when I unlocked the door and let him and his crew in."

"I think I'll run next door and invite them to eat lunch with us. Lord knows I brought enough food for half a dozen people." Birdie headed for the storage room. "I'll need my coat and umbrella."

"If you're going to invite them all for lunch, just use the telephone," Lori Lee suggested as she strolled around the shop, flicking imaginary specks of dust off the countertops. "And if Rick accepts, I hope y'all have a lovely lunch. Unfortunately, I won't be here."

"What do you mean, you won't be here?"

"I mean I'll go somewhere else for lunch. I will not allow you to play matchmaker for me with a man who is as unsuitable for me as I am for him."

Birdie pivoted around slowly, then smiled broadly when

she glanced at the front door. "You do whatever you want, sugar, but I'm going to issue my invitation in person."

Lori Lee followed her aunt's mesmerized stare, straight to the man approaching the front entrance. When the door opened, a blustery wind blew a gust of frozen rain into the shop as Rick Warrick entered. He shook the rain from his shaggy black hair and brushed icy droplets off his thick, corduroy work jacket. Lori Lee noticed the swirl of dark chest hair peeping over the top of his beige thermal undershirt.

"Good day, ladies."

The sound of his deep, husky voice rippled along Lori Lee's nerve endings like Mississippi sorghum poured over hot flapjacks.

"Well, hello, Rick," Aunt Birdie said. "You boys taking a lunch break? Because if you are, Lori Lee and I would like to invite you to share lunch with us. I brought leftovers from my Sunday dinner."

"Thank you, Miss Birdie—"

"Aunt Birdie."

"Thank you, Aunt Birdie. I'm sure your leftovers will beat the heck out of my cold bologna sandwich." Rick ran his fingers through his damp hair. "I'd be happy to accept your offer, if we can postpone eating for a bit."

"Wonderful." Birdie beamed, her eyelashes fluttered. "How long shall we wait? It's nearly noon. I thought y'all took your lunch break at twelve."

"We do, and my men are getting ready to eat right now. But before I join you ladies for lunch, I'd like y'all to come next door for a minute."

"Is something wrong?" Lori Lee asked. "Have y'all run into a problem of some sort in removing the old heating system?"

"No, ma'am, not a problem, just an interesting development," Rick said. "While we were tearing out the old heating unit, a part of the wooden wall behind it fell in. The boards were rotted clean through."

"Was it some type of support wall?" Lori Lee went into the basement as seldom as possible. She hated the creepy feeling it gave her, as if she were inside a tomb. "Is there any danger of the upper level floor falling in?"

"No, nothing like that," Rick assured her. "The wall served no purpose, really. I figure it was put up to close off part of the basement. We found something down there I thought you and Miss...Aunt Birdie might like to see."

"Something in our basement?" Dimples creased Birdie's fat cheeks. "Well, you go on over, sugar, and check it out. I'm afraid I can't get up and down those rickety old stairs." She smiled at Rick. "Just what have you found?"

"It looks like a bar," Rick said. "And not just any bar. This sucker is a huge, ornately carved wooden bar, a good fifteen feet long."

"Oh, my, yes." Birdie clapped her hands together like a giddy child. "I've heard the rumors all my life, but I never realized that the old speakeasy was located in the basement of one of my buildings. Isn't this exciting?"

Lori Lee didn't know whether she would call the discovery of an old bar beneath her studio exciting or not, but Aunt Birdie and Rick certainly seemed to think so. She really wasn't interested in exploring the subterranean depths beneath Tuscumbia, but if she didn't pacify Aunt Birdie's curiosity, her elderly aunt just might try to make the journey into the basement herself.

"All right. Let's go see this great marvel." Lori Lee wondered if she'd need her jacket. But if she took the time to bundle up and get an umbrella it would only prolong this little adventure. "We'll be back in just a few minutes."

"Take your time," Birdie called after them as they rushed out the door.

The awnings connecting the two buildings partially protected them from the downpour, but not from the wind gusts. Rick flung the door open for her, then followed her inside. Several workers spoke or nodded to Lori Lee; she returned their greetings. The men sat on the floor, their lunches spread out around them like a picnic.

"It's quite a sight, Miss Guy. Bet that bar's been in the basement since the twenties," one of the crew members said. "After lunch we'll clean up all that old rotted wood before we do anything else."

Rick placed his hand in the small of Lori Lee's back and guided her down the basement steps. His hand was big and warm and strong. His touch seared her through her sweater.

No other man's touch had ever affected her the way Rick's did. Years after he'd grabbed her on the front porch when she was seventeen, she'd told herself that she had exaggerated the power of his touch, that memories often played tricks on a person's emotions. But this touch wasn't memory. It was here and now—and its power was as great as she remembered.

She hurried down the steps, fleeing from him, trying to escape the unwanted sensations spiraling up from the depths of her femininity. The chill of the damp basement hit her suddenly. She shivered. Hugging her body to warm herself, she rubbed her palms up and down her arms.

"Are you cold?" Rick asked, coming up behind her.

"Yes," she admitted. "I should have brought my coat."

Before she could utter a protest, he removed his jacket and flung it around her shoulders. As she turned to face him, he pulled the zippered edge across her chest. His hands lingered, his long, thick fingers clutching the material. His knuckles rested in the crevice between her breasts.

Lori Lee looked at his hands. Big and broad. The tops sprinkled with dark hair. The palms callused.

"Thank you. But won't you be cold without it?" She lifted her gaze to his face and her breath caught in her throat. Didn't the man ever shave? Or was it that his heavy black beard gave him a perpetual five-o'clock shadow?

A lock of hair hung across the edge of his forehead. She longed to brush the errant strand away from his eye. She clenched her hand into a tight fist, warning herself not to touch him.

"I'm tough," he said. "I'll be fine."

He didn't have to tell her how tough he was. She knew—everyone knew. Fifteen years ago, he'd been the toughest kid in town. Everyone, even the young hoods who didn't have sense enough to be afraid, steered clear of Rick Warrick. Perhaps even they'd sensed what Lori Lee had—that Rick had a death wish, creating a wild, reckless fearlessness in him.

Even at thirty-three, he still possessed an aura of strength that warned others away. It was as if he wore a sign stating Trespass At Your Own Risk.

"Where's the bar?" she asked. "I need to take a look at it and report back to Aunt Birdie."

Releasing the jacket, he reached down and grabbed her hand. "Come on. It's back here. Be careful. Step over the shards of wood there." He nodded to the floor.

Pulling a small flashlight out of his back pocket, he flipped it on and pointed the beam through the huge opening in the flimsy wooden wall. Rick maneuvered around the debris on the floor, guiding her safely into the mouth of the hole. Lori Lee hesitated.

"Hey, there's nothing to be afraid of down here," he told her, grinning in his cocky, masculine way.

"I know there isn't. I just don't like dark, closed-in places, especially underground."

"Then we won't stay long. Just take a quick look at the bar and I'll get you back upstairs."

Holding his hand tightly, she allowed him to guide her into the once sealed-off section of the basement. He flashed the light directly on the bar. Lori Lee gasped. She truly never would have believed it if she hadn't seen it with her own two eyes. Dirty, dust and cobweb covered, the huge bar rested along the side of the brick wall. An enormous, cracked, gilt-framed mirror hung above it.

"This is incredible." Lori Lee stared at the bar, her

mouth open, her blue eyes wide. "Aunt Birdie must be right about a speakeasy having been in this basement during prohibition."

"Just imagine the stories that bar could tell if it could talk," Rick said. "All the fun times, the wild parties, the loud music, the sexy women. Think how many upstanding citizens drove down Main Street, up there—" Rick nodded his head toward the ceiling "—on their way to church on Sunday morning, after having committed more than their share of sins down here the Saturday night before."

"Knowing Aunt Birdie's penchant for the unorthodox, I wouldn't put it past her to fix things up down here and turn it into a tourist attraction."

"I doubt the city council would allow it."

"Tuscumbia is not nearly as old-fashioned and narrow-minded as you think," Lori Lee assured him. "Besides, as obsessed as everyone here is with history, I can't believe they'd turn their backs on this part of the city's past."

"Think what you will, honey, but I'd lay odds against this town agreeing to show off the remains of a speakeasy."

"If you think so little of our town, why did you come back here?"

Fifteen years ago Rick couldn't leave Colbert County fast enough, couldn't put enough miles between him and Tuscumbia, Alabama. He had hated being an outcast, a misfit the townspeople had never accepted. When he'd been a kid, he'd wanted what his little sister had—foster parents who eventually adopted her. But he'd been ten when his mother died and already labeled as a bad seed. He'd heard people whispering about him, predicting that he'd turn out to be as worthless as his father had been. And by the age of eighteen, he had proved them right.

But he was a man now, thirty-three, with all his wild oats sown. He had a child depending on him, and more than anything, he wanted to make a place for Darcie in this community.

"I think Tuscumbia is as good or bad as any other small

Southern town," Rick said. "Probably more good than bad. That's why I came back. I wanted Darcie to grow up here, close to her aunt and cousins. I want her to have friends, be accepted."

"The way you weren't?" Lori Lee didn't mean to touch him. Her fingertips seemed to have a life of their own as she reached up and caressed his cheek.

He grabbed her hand, covering it with his own, holding its soft warmth against his face. "Feeling sorry for me, honey?"

"Maybe, just a little. But mostly I'm remembering what a loner you used to be and how, when I'd see you at school or on the street, I'd wonder what was going on inside you. You acted like you didn't need anybody."

Rick eased his arm around her waist, up under his jacket that she wore. His fingers slipped beneath the hem of her pink turtleneck sweater and spread gently across her naked back. "I learned at an early age not to need anyone and not to show weakness of any kind. People looked down on me because my old man had been a worthless drifter and my mother was white trash. When the Mayfields adopted Eve, she became acceptable. I wasn't so lucky."

Lori Lee shivered involuntarily, not from the chill in the basement, but from the excitement of his touch. She wanted to take him in her arms, hold him close and kiss away yesterday's pain. The pain of a lost and lonely little boy no one had wanted. "You always fascinated me," she admitted. "I heard people talking about you. They said some pretty terrible things. I didn't want to believe what they said was true, but you never gave me or anyone else a chance to believe in you."

Rick caressed her back, his palm warm and hard on her delicate skin. She gasped as purely sensual sensations tingled along her nerve endings.

"Don't think I didn't want you back then, honey. You were the sweetest temptation I'd ever know." He cupped her hip with his other hand, drawing her intimately close.

Her breath came in quick, heated gasps. ''You were everything I wanted, and everything I couldn't have. Scaring you off that night I showed up at the Debutante party was probably the noblest thing I ever did.''

She placed her hands on his chest, intending to push him away. Words of protest formed in her mind. She shouldn't allow him to touch her this way or say these things to her. She was inviting trouble that she had no idea how to handle. Rick Warrick wasn't like other men. On the surface he might be a reformed sinner, but something told Lori Lee that underneath his newly formed civilized facade, the wild and wicked Rick still existed.

''You didn't scare me off.'' Her fingers spread apart on his chest, her palms tingling. ''The night you kissed me on the front porch, I would have followed you anywhere, even to hell. Even after you shoved me away and warned me against you, I would have given you anything you wanted. But you made it clear you didn't want me, so I ran away. But a few minutes later, I worked up enough courage to go back outside and look for you. Mary Dru Sparkman was waiting for you in her car. I—I saw the two of you. I—''

''Yeah, I know, honey. I wanted you to see us. I thought you needed to know that I was the kind of guy who had no qualms about going from kissing your sweet, innocent lips to making out with a little tramp like Mary Dru.''

''You did it on purpose, didn't you?'' Lori Lee gripped his shoulders. ''I figured it out, years later.''

''Sometimes, I wish I hadn't been so damned noble.'' He pulled her into his arms, crushing her breasts into his chest, pressing her against his growing hardness. ''I should have taken you with me that night and said to hell with your innocence and to hell with the barriers that stood between us.''

Lori Lee pulsated deep in the secret heart of her body. Longings more intense than any she'd ever known radiated through her. She eased her hands up his chest, over his shoulders and around his neck. "I've always wondered what it would have been like with you."

"I'd have been your first, if I'd taken you that night." The words were a statement, not a question. All the guys had known that Lori Lee Guy didn't put out, that she was waiting for Prince Charming.

A thousand times since that night, she'd wished that Rick Warrick had been her first lover. Her wedding night had been a disappointment, despite how much she loved her husband. Tory had been quite experienced at having sex, but knew very little about making love. As time passed, their love life improved and she'd been happy. Then she discovered Tory's many infidelities shortly after her third miscarriage. At the lowest point in her life, her husband had destroyed her self-confidence and undermined her worth as a woman.

"I wish—" Standing on tiptoe, Lori Lee gazed up at Rick. Her eyes filled with a desire she could not disguise, and she whispered against his lips, "I wish you had been my first lover."

Blazing heat waves followed by cold, jarring shocks pelted Rick's body. Of all the things for her to have said to him, why that? Dear God in heaven, didn't she know what her admission was doing to him? For fifteen years, hers had been the image of perfection he had carried in his heart. Every woman he'd known had fallen short of his idealized lover. He'd lost track of the women in his past, before and after his brief marriage to April. But the one woman he'd never been able to forget was the one woman he'd never made love to—except in his dreams.

When they'd been teenagers, he hadn't been good enough for her. Their social positions, her innocence, his insecurities and his stupid sense of chivalry when it came to Lori Lee had kept them apart. Now, all these years later, he still wasn't good enough for her. But at this precise moment, he really didn't give a damn.

Later, neither of them knew who had actually instigated

the kiss. It seemed to have happened spontaneously. He lowered his mouth—she lifted hers. And the world around them vanished. The damp, dark basement. The cold winter sleet outside. The workmen on their lunch break upstairs. Nothing and no one existed except the two of them and their hot, wild, uncontrollable lust.

He had remembered that long-ago kiss, had lived off the memory for fifteen years, had even thought his mind had exaggerated the importance of it. But as he took her mouth, forcefully shoving his tongue inside, he knew the memory didn't do justice to the reality. This was what a kiss was meant to be—so powerful it propelled a man to the edge of release.

She accepted his invasion, her own tongue pushing against his, seeking and finding the wet heat it craved. Rick cupped her buttocks, kneading them with gentle strength through the pink wool of her slacks. Her body tightened, moistened, throbbed. She clung to him, kissing him with mindless passion. Wanting. Needing. Longing for more. So much more.

He loved the way she moaned into his mouth. Sweet little cries of need. He wanted her naked beneath him, her wet, tight body milking him of his last ounce of strength. If he didn't end this now, before he lost complete control, he would take her in the dark, dank basement. Against the damp wall. On the hard dirt floor. Or on the rickety wooden steps.

He ended the kiss by slow degrees. Removing his tongue, he licked her lips, then nibbled on her soft flesh. She opened her eyes, their expression dreamy.

"Rick?" With her arms draped around his neck, she rubbed against him, like a cat curling around its master's leg.

"I want you so bad I'm dying." He gave her a hard, quick kiss, then grabbed her shoulders and pushed her a few feet away from his aching body. "I could take you, right here, right now. God knows I want to. But do you want our first time to be here? Like this?''

"Our first time," she repeated the words, her voice a dazed whisper. "I...I...oh, Rick, I don't know what happened to me."

"To us, honey. It happened to us. And I know exactly what happened. We touched each other and ignited a fire. It's going to happen every time we're together. You might as well accept that fact, and deal with it." He dropped his hands from her shoulders, but his gaze held her captive.

"This shouldn't have happened," Lori Lee said, her voice quivering slightly. "It's my fault. I'm not blaming you. The truth is that I wanted you even though..."

"Are you trying to tell me that your body wants mine, but your mind warns you against me?"

Her body had warmed with desire, her face hotly flushed. She'd made a terrible mistake giving in to her emotions.

"Rick, I'm not the right woman for you." He wanted and needed a woman capable of giving him more children—she could never be that woman. "And you're not the right man for me." She knew exactly what most of her female friends would say about A. K. Warrick. They'd tell her to have a discreet affair with him and work him out of her system, but God forbid that she marry him. He wasn't their kind. He had come from nothing, and was still struggling to overcome his heritage therefore certain people considered the man himself nothing.

"The bottom line is that I'm not good enough for you." His voice possessed a cold, bitter edge. "I never have been, and no matter what, I never will be."

"That isn't true," she said, all the while she could hear other people's voices repeating his statement. *Rick Warrick isn't good enough for someone like Lori Lee Guy. Not good enough. Not good enough.* But she knew the truth. She was the one who wasn't good enough. She could never be enough woman for Rick because she was only half a woman. Barren. Childless. Her body incapable of a woman's most basic function—giving birth.

"Deny it all you want, honey." He grabbed her by the arm, his dark eyes glaring at her. "But we both know it's how you feel. How most of this town feels. And it's true. I can work my fingers to the bone. I can become a successful businessman. I can prove myself a good father. But people aren't going to forget who I was and what I came from, are they?"

She looked at him pleadingly. "That's not true. Just because you and I can't have a relationship doesn't mean you aren't good enough for me."

"Yeah, sure." He jerked on her arm. "Let's get out of here. I'm sure your Aunt Birdie is eager to hear all about our discovery."

"Rick, please—"

He halted abruptly, releasing his hold on her. "Please what? Please stop wanting you? Please stop comparing every woman I meet to you? Please stop breathing?"

"Please forgive me." Forgive me for not being woman enough for you. Forgive me for not having the courage to reach out and take what I want and not care what my friends think. And forgive me for being so afraid.

She ran from him, rushing up the steps and not looking back. Once upstairs, she nodded to the workmen who spoke to her as she hurried out of the studio and into the icy slush. She didn't realize she still wore Rick's jacket until she was inside the Sparkle and Shine shop.

"Well, my goodness gracious. From the looks of you, I'd say Rick's discovery in the basement was a rather exciting experience for you." Birdie gazed at her niece with knowing green eyes, a gleeful grin on her face. "Or perhaps taking a look at the old speakeasy bar has nothing to do with that sexual flush on your cheeks."

"Don't you dare start in with me, Birdie Pierpont!" Lori Lee ripped off Rick's jacket and threw it at her aunt. Birdie caught it before it hit the floor. "Give that to Mr. Warrick, if he bothers to come after it.'' Lori Lee stormed into the back storage room and slammed the door.

Alone, Lori Lee slumped down into a chair at her work desk, covered her face with her hands and cried silently. What had happened today in the studio basement could never happen again. If it did, she wasn't sure she'd have the strength to walk away, and something told her that next time Rick wouldn't call a halt to their lovemaking.

Four

Lori Lee hadn't spoken to Rick since their passionate encounter in the basement, and she'd seen him only at a distance. Although Rick's sister brought Darcie to practice and often picked her up, Rick had managed to pick up his daughter twice. And he'd been late both times. Since he worked from eight till five, there was no reason he couldn't get to the studio by six-thirty, right after Darcie's class ended. What did he do during that hour and a half that delayed him?

Lori Lee had told herself she didn't care what Rick did and with whom he did it. She was not going to get involved with a man who could mean nothing but trouble for her. He might claim to be trying to reform, but Lori Lee doubted his ability to change. Of course, whether or not Rick was a new man really didn't matter. She was the same woman who had miscarried three babies and been told she could never have a child of her own.

In the weeks since meeting Darcie Warrick, Lori Lee had

guarded her emotions, knowing how easy it would be for her to love Rick's little girl. "My name's Darcie Lee," the child had informed her. "We've got the same middle name, don't we?"

She had wondered if Rick had named his daughter after her. Was it truly possible that he'd cared about her all these years? She certainly hadn't been able to forget him. When her marriage had begun to fall apart, she had thought more and more about Rick, often fantasizing that he was the one making love to her instead of Tory.

"Hey, girl, where'd you go off to?" Deanie Webber punched Lori Lee on the arm.

Gasping, Lori Lee came out of her private thoughts and smiled sadly. "Just thinking about Darcie."

"Look, I'll be glad to take her home since Rick's running a little late," Deanie said. "It's not much out of my way."

"No, that won't be necessary. I'm sure Rick will be here soon. He's usually late."

"Maybe he runs late on purpose so he can talk to you for a few minutes without so many twirler mothers hanging around undressing him with their eyes."

Lori Lee chuckled. "You and Aunt Birdie have a knack for cutting to the chase and saying just what you think." She sighed. "But you're wrong about Rick's reason for being late. He doesn't come in and talk to me. He meets Darcie outside."

"So what happened to scare him off?" Deanie asked. "What did you do, lie to him and tell him you weren't interested?"

"I'm not interested." Lori Lee crossed her arms over her chest.

"Yeah, sure. And I don't cheat on my diet. Get real. This is Deanie you're talking to."

"Rick and I agreed that we aren't suitable." Lori Lee lowered her voice to a soft murmur when Darcie and Katie Webber came bounding down the stairs.

"Look at us, Lori Lee," Katie said. "I've been practicing our Twinkle Toes dance routine with Darcie just like you asked me to do."

"We'll discuss this later," Deanie whispered to Lori Lee, then turned her attention toward the two six-year-olds in hot-pink tights and black leotards who were eagerly waiting to perform. "Go ahead, girls. Show us your routine."

"You won't believe how good Darcie is," Katie said. "She's going to do great when we go to Clanton."

"Well, let's see what you two can do." Lori Lee focused her attention on Rick's daughter, on the adorable blue-eyed blonde who seemed to worship her. The child obviously needed and wanted a mother, and for some reason she had chosen Lori Lee. Perhaps it was because so many people had commented about the striking resemblance between the two of them. And more than one twirler mother had commented on how talented Darcie was, having taken lessons only a month and already upstaging some of the more seasoned students.

Watching Darcie and Katie perform the dance she had choreographed to the song "Singing in the Rain," from the old MGM Gene Kelly movie, Lori Lee smiled proudly at how well the two girls did the number. People were right. Darcie Warrick possessed a natural talent for dancing, twirling and showmanship, the way Lori Lee always had.

A feeling like none she'd ever known swirled up inside of Lori Lee, clutching her heart, misting her eyes with tears and taunting her with irrational thoughts. *This little girl— Rick's daughter—is mine.* For some reason fate had played a horrible trick on her by giving the child that was meant to be hers to another woman.

Deanie's loud clapping brought Lori Lee quickly back to reality. She applauded with great enthusiasm, then rushed over and hugged both girls. Darcie clung to her, hugging her fiercely, as if she never wanted to let her go.

"Y'all were wonderful," Lori Lee told them.

Katie ran to Deanie, who kissed her child's cheek. "I

swear, you are the best little girl in the whole world. You got my looks and your dad's brains.'' Katie giggled at her mother's playfully loving comments.

As Lori Lee stood, Darcie grabbed her hand and gazed up at her with a pleading look that asked for recognition.

Dear God! Lori Lee closed her eyes, blinking back the tears as she fought and gained control of her emotions. Her instincts told her to claim this child, to give Darcie Warrick exactly what she wanted—a mother. But she couldn't do that. It would be wrong. Wrong for Darcie. And wrong for her.

Lori Lee cupped Darcie's chin with her hand. ''Your father will be so proud of you, sweetheart. When he picks you up today, I'm going to ask him if you can perform the Halftime Show Dance Line routine with our Twinkle Toes group when we go to Clanton.''

Darcie jumped up and down. Katie followed suit. Within minutes both girls were clapping their hands and squealing with childish glee.

''Am I really that good, Lori Lee?'' Darcie asked.

''You're really that good,'' Lori Lee said. ''And if you continue to practice, I have no doubt you'll be ready to move into Twinkle Toes and compete in all their events by the end of summer.''

''Well, I hate to leave when we're having such a good time,'' Deanie said. ''But Phil will be home soon and he's taking us out for dinner.'' Deanie lifted her child's coat off the rack and held it out for her. ''Come on, Katie. We've got to go.'' Deanie glanced at her watch, then at Lori Lee. ''It's ten till seven. Are you sure you don't want me to drop Darcie by Eve's?''

''No, thanks. If Rick isn't here soon, I'll take Darcie home myself.''

''Good idea.'' Deanie winked mischievously at Lori Lee as she helped Katie into her coat. ''I'll expect a full report.''

"There will be nothing to report," Lori Lee called after Deanie as she and Katie waved goodbye.

Darcie tugged on Lori Lee's hand. "I'm sorry my daddy's late. Sometimes he takes a nap after he gets home from work. He works very hard and gets tired."

Lori Lee nodded as if she understood, but in truth, she was upset that Rick could be so irresponsible. Other parents, some also single, managed to pick up their children on time. Why couldn't he?

"Do you know if your Aunt Eve is home?" Lori Lee asked.

"Aunt Eve's probably at her ceramic class right now, and Uncle Tommy's baby-sitting," Darcie said. "That means tonight is hamburger night and Uncle Tommy's cooking. I like his hamburgers, but they're not as good as my daddy's."

"Well, it looks like *something* has delayed your father." Lori Lee removed Darcie's coat and her own from the wall rack. "I'll run you home. I want to talk to your father."

Lori Lee helped Darcie into her coat, then slipped into her own. She retrieved her shoulder bag from the desk, turned off the lights and opened the front door.

Once they were settled inside Lori Lee's white Buick Riviera, Darcie said, "My daddy's not married, you know."

"Yes, I know." Lori Lee inserted the key in the ignition and started the car.

"He dates. Aunt Eve's been trying to find him a wife, but he hasn't dated anybody we want to keep."

Lori Lee smiled despite her best efforts not to. "Is that right?"

"Yeah. Aunt Eve says that Daddy's too hard to please. But he told her that he wasn't going to marry just anybody. He wants to find somebody special that we'll both love."

"I'm sure your father will find the right woman one of these days." Lori Lee couldn't believe she was actually discussing Rick's love life with his six-year-old daughter.

"You aren't married are you, Lori Lee?" Darcie asked.

Lori Lee knew where this conversation was headed if she didn't steer it in another direction. "No, I'm not married, but I already have several boyfriends."

"Wouldn't you like to have one more?"

Lori Lee was both touched and amused by Darcie's matchmaking scheme. Heaven help her and Rick if the child ever joined forces with Aunt Birdie.

"I don't know how I'd make time for another boyfriend," Lori Lee said, trying desperately to keep a straight face.

"Couldn't you get rid of one of your other boyfriends and make room for somebody new?"

"Look, we're here already." Lori Lee pulled her Riviera into Eve Nelson's double driveway. Rick's sister's house was on East Sixth Street, just a few minutes' drive from downtown. Glad for an excuse not to have to answer Darcie's question, Lori Lee unbuckled her seat belt, then reached over and undid Darcie's.

"I'll go tell Uncle Tommy I'm home, while you go up to our apartment and talk to Daddy. You can tell him I'll fix him a hamburger and have it ready for him." Darcie opened the car door, then glanced back at Lori Lee. "I'm sure it would be all right if you wanted to stay and eat with us."

"Oh. Well, it's awfully nice of you to invite me, but I'm afraid I can't stay. Not tonight."

"Sometime soon, maybe?"

"Maybe."

"I'll get Aunt Eve to call you." Before Lori Lee could respond, Darcie jumped out of the car and dashed into the house. Lori Lee got out, walked straight up the driveway to the garage apartment and climbed the steps. Backyard floodlights illuminated the Nelsons' yard and house, as well as the large detached garage and upstairs apartment.

Lori Lee had wondered if she'd find Rick at home. His

old GMC pickup truck was parked in the garage below, so she assumed he was here.

She knocked on the front door. No answer. She knocked again. Harder. Louder. Still no reply. She tried the door-knob, and to her surprise the door opened. Easing inside, she glanced around at the small, rather dismal room. A compact stove, refrigerator, sink and several cabinets lined the pale green right wall. The furnishings were sparse. There was a card table and four folding chairs near the kitchen alcove, and a well-worn, olive green sofa and matching rocker in the living room area. Two mismatched lamps, both burning brightly, sat atop a couple of old pine end tables. Miniblinds covered the windows.

"Rick?" she called out to him. "Where are you?"

There were three doors from which to choose. One was partially open and she could tell it was a tiny bathroom. Another was to her left and the final one straight in front of her. She picked the door in front of her, opening it to discover a small bedroom painted a pale shade of blue and decorated with a tiny floral print perfect for a little girl. Eve Nelson must have put together the precious room for her niece.

"Rick! Are you here? I brought Darcie home."

Turning to the left, she opened the third door and found a dark place not much larger than the bathroom. The light from the living room cast wavy gray shadows into the area. A bed without a headboard had been pushed up against the wall and took up most of the floor space. Rick Warrick, still wearing his navy blue work coveralls, lay sprawled out across the bed, snoring loudly.

What was wrong with him? Was he sick? Drunk? She leaned over, called his name and shook him gently. He grabbed her wrist and hauled her down on top of him. Lori Lee cried out, partly in surprise and partly in fear. The man lying beneath her was big and hard and very strong. Her heartbeat accelerated at a maddening speed.

He blinked his eyes several times and stared up into her

face. "Lori Lee?" His voice was deep and groggy. He closed his eyes. "Dreaming," he whispered the word against her lips.

She trembled. "Rick. You're not dreaming. Wake up."

He bound her tightly to him, caressing her hip and thigh. She moaned softly, her body instinctively softening into his.

His eyes flew open. He shot straight up into a sitting position, almost knocking Lori Lee off the bed. Grabbing her around the waist, he pulled her onto his lap.

"What the hell are you doing here?" He growled the question.

As always, he badly needed a shave and a haircut. And as always, he looked incredibly handsome and sexy. "I brought Darcie home. It's seven o'clock. You forgot to pick her up at the studio."

"Oh, God, Lori Lee, I'm sorry. I set my alarm, but the damned thing didn't go off."

She jumped up, placed her hands on her hips and glared at Rick. "We need to talk."

He grabbed the clock, shook it and groaned. "I'll have to get some new batteries." Standing, he rubbed his bristly chin and yawned. "Where's Darcie?"

"She's fixing you a hamburger over at your sister's house," Lori Lee said, backing away from him. "I understand this is Uncle Tommy's night to cook."

"Yeah, Tommy's great with kids. His two and Darcie. I don't know what I'd do without his and Eve's help." Rick moved toward her, backing her against the wall. "It isn't easy raising a kid alone."

"Other people seem to manage." Lori Lee shoved against Rick's chest, but he didn't budge. "You're always late picking her up and today is a prime example of what an irresponsible father you are. Why do you need a nap in the afternoon? It wouldn't be because you're out carousing around all night, would it? From what Darcie has said, I get the idea she spends several nights a week at her Aunt Eve's.''

When Rick backed away from Lori Lee, she escaped into the living room. Standing in the doorway, Rick snorted and shook his head. His accusing stare bored into her.

"You've condemned me without a trial, haven't you, honey? Once an irresponsible hell-raiser, always an irresponsible hell-raiser. Is that the way you see it?''

"Am I wrong?'' Gripping her leather shoulder bag, she glared at him.

"How could you possibly be wrong about anything? You're Lori Lee Guy.''

"I can't understand why you'd leave that precious child to go out tomcatting around at night when you could be at home with her. If she were mine—''

"But she's not yours,'' Rick said. "She's mine, and for your information—'' He stopped talking midsentence. "No, you go ahead and think what you want to think, believe what you want to believe.''

"I wanted to believe, for Darcie's sake, that you'd changed.''

He took a step toward her. She backed away. He continued walking toward her until he forced her into the open doorway leading to the small wooden stoop at the top of the stairs.

"You want to think I'm still the town bad boy who isn't worthy to kiss your feet.'' Rick grasped Lori Lee's shoulders, his big fingers biting into her tender flesh. "You're looking for a reason not to like me, to think the worst of me. It makes it easier to reject me if you can convince yourself that I'm not a decent person.''

"That's not true.'' Lori Lee realized he was going to kiss her and knew she was powerless to stop him.

The kiss was fast, forceful and almost brutal. A kiss of anger as much as of passion. She felt the powerful effect from her spinning head to her weak knees.

Releasing her, Rick stepped back into his apartment. The

light from inside the living room silhouetted his big body. Lori Lee looked at him, uncertainty and longing waging a war inside her. Uncertainty won. She turned and fled, running down the stairs and out to her car.

Lori Lee curled up on the sofa and sipped the cinnamon spice tea she'd poured into one of her good china cups. Tyke lay at her side, snoring. She ran her hand over his little head and down his neck. He grunted, turned over on his back, his feet in the air, and continued sleeping.

Lori Lee laughed, envying her dog's easy life. "You've got it made, buddy boy, and you don't even know it."

When she'd come home tonight, she had taken a long bubble bath, eaten a light salad, then put on a classical music CD. Whenever she felt especially lonely or sad, she treated herself to little creature comforts she found so consoling.

Her encounter with Rick had been more than unpleasant; it had been frightening. Not that she thought Rick would harm her physically. No, she knew he wasn't that type of man. But his ability to harm her emotionally could not be dismissed lightly. Her foolish attraction to him posed a threat not only to her sanity, but to her safe, secure, orderly life. She'd be a fool to trust him. She doubted he'd ever been faithful to a woman in his entire life.

And her emotional involvement with his daughter created problems for her she wasn't sure she could handle. As much as she loved all children, she found herself drawn to Darcie Warrick more than any other child. Perhaps because she recognized the need in Darcie, the hungry longing for a mother, just as Lori Lee's maternal instincts called out for a child of her own.

Maybe she needed another dog. Or even a cat. Aunt Birdie had two dogs and four cats, and treated them all like spoiled children. Lori Lee had bought Tyke four years ago when he was three months old. She had wanted to have someone waiting for her when she came home. Someone to keep her company. Someone besides other people's children on which to lavish her love and attention.

The doorbell rang. Gasping, Lori Lee jumped. Who on earth? Glancing at the mantel clock, she noted it was after nine o'clock. She got up, tightened the belt around her black velvet robe and went to the door. Peering through the viewfinder, she saw Eve Nelson standing on her front porch. Although puzzled by the woman's unexpected visit, Lori Lee opened the door and greeted her guest with a smile.

"Please, come in, Eve," Lori Lee said.

"Thanks." Eve walked into the small marble-floored foyer. "I apologize for not calling first, but I felt it was important that we talk, face-to-face, and I was afraid if I called first, you might not see me."

"May I take your coat and purse?"

"No. I won't be here long." Eve unbuttoned her beige wool coat.

"All right. Why don't we go into the den?" Lori Lee motioned the direction with a sweep of her hand. "I was just having a cup of cinnamon tea. Would you care for some?"

"No, thank you." Eve followed Lori Lee into her warm, cozy den, decorated in an eclectic fashion. Antiques blended with several secondhand store finds—new mixed beautifully with old.

"What's wrong, Eve? You seem upset." Lori Lee sat on the sofa, then indicated for her guest to be seated.

Eve shook her head. "No, I'd rather stand. I probably have no right to be here, but after Rick told me what happened, I felt I had no choice."

"I'm sorry, but I have no idea what you're talking about." Lori Lee gazed quizzically at Eve. "Exactly what did Rick tell you?"

"He said that he overslept and didn't pick up Darcie from twirler practice, so you brought her home." Eve wrung her hands repeatedly and shifted her weight from one foot to the other and then back again. "When you brought her home, you chewed him out and told him he was an irresponsible father. You even accused him of staying out all night, tomcatting around."

"He didn't deny it." Had Rick sent his sister here to defend him? If he was innocent, if he had an explanation for his actions, why hadn't he come himself to confront her?

"I cannot believe you accused him of such a thing, or that you could actually believe Rick is an irresponsible father. His whole world revolves around Darcie. Everything he's doing, he's doing for her."

"I don't doubt that Rick loves his child, but his actions indicate a lack of responsibility. Whenever he picks her up at the studio, he's always late, and today he didn't even show up."

"He tries to catch a nap every evening. His alarm didn't go off today."

"If he stayed home at night he wouldn't need an afternoon nap, would he?"

"You're wrong if you think Rick wants to be gone at night. He'd much rather be home with Darcie, but—"

"But what?" Lori Lee interrupted, nervous and agitated at the realization she might have misjudged Rick. "If he's not out tomcatting around at night, why would he need a nap in the evening?"

"Because he works two jobs," Eve said. "At seventhirty, four nights a week, he leaves Darcie at my house and goes to a garage he rented up on North Main. He's restoring a '59 Corvette for your friend, Powell Goodman. Rick doesn't get in until after midnight and he's up at five every morning to do the laundry, clean the apartment and fix breakfast."

"He's working two jobs?" Lori Lee asked, an incredulous look in her eyes. "But why?"

"Because he wants to take out a loan to buy Bobo Lewis's half of the business when Bobo retires. He used his entire life savings to buy into the business to start with, and now he'll have to borrow a substantial amount of money. He needs as much up front as he can possibly earn.''

A sad, heart-wrenching realization came over Lori Lee. She understood Rick's reasoning without Eve explaining any further. ''He wants to be a respected businessman so that people here in Tuscumbia will accept Darcie.''

Tears welled up in Eve's brown eyes. ''I've never seen a man try so hard. This need he has to give Darcie everything he wanted and never had is eating away at him. You have no idea what a financial burden it is on him to pay for Darcie's lessons and buy her costumes. And...'' Eve hesitated as if carefully considering what she was going to say. ''You can't imagine how much your opinion of him matters.''

''How could I have been so stupid? Oh, Eve, I said some terrible things to him. You have every right to be upset with me. I'm glad you came over and set me straight. I owe Rick an apology.''

''Yes, you do.'' Eve sighed, then smiled weakly. ''I don't want you or anyone else thinking badly of Rick, assuming he's the way he used to be. He's changed a lot because of Darcie. He's trying to be a good father. Your accusations were totally unfounded.''

''I appreciate your talking so honestly with me,'' Lori Lee said. ''I promise that I'll speak to him. I'll apologize.''

''Thanks, Lori Lee. Rick needs all the support he can get, but especially from people like you.''

''What do you mean, people like me?''

''People he used to know years ago who always looked down on him.''

''I never...'' Lori Lee didn't finish her sentence, realizing that she *had* been a part of the crowd who'd indeed looked down their noses at Rick and other people like him. And she was still a part of that same crowd. ''I want Rick to succeed, and I'll do whatever I can to help see that Darcie is accepted by the other girls.''

''She's crazy about you, you know.'' Eve nervously adjusted her shoulder bag. ''She talks about you all the time. You've helped her already, more than you know.''

''I'm very fond of Darcie,'' Lori Lee admitted. *And I could easily love her far more than would be good for either of us.*

''I need to be going. I appreciate your understanding of the situation. Please continue being a good friend to Darcie. And...well, be Rick's friend, too, if you can.''

''Thanks for coming by.'' Standing, Lori Lee smiled graciously at Rick's sister. ''I'll walk out with you.''

Lori Lee stood on the front porch until Eve hopped in her Bronco and started the engine, then she went back inside and locked the front door. Hesitating in the foyer, she suddenly realized what she wanted to do—what she had to do. She was going to see Rick tonight and tell him how sorry she was for jumping to all the wrong conclusions. Even if they could never be anything more, maybe they could be friends. She had a feeling that Rick didn't make friends easily, and if there was one thing he could use in this town, it was someone in her crowd to befriend him and his child.

The concrete block garage on North Main Street had once been a service station back in the sixties. Now, with peeling paint, broken windows and grass growing through the cracks in the driveway, the place appeared deserted except for the light on inside. Lori Lee parked her Riviera in front, then got out and glanced up and down the street. It was nearly ten o'clock. Most people were snug in their warm homes, no one anywhere around to wonder what Lori Lee Guy was doing out alone on North Main late at night. The cold February wind whipped through Lori Lee's jeans. Hurrying to the entrance, she tried the handle and found the door locked. She pounded her gloved fist against the metal door.

She had argued with herself over the pros and cons of seeking Rick out tonight. She could have waited until tomorrow and called him. That would have been the sensible thing to do. But when it came to Rick Warrick, she found it difficult to always be sensible.

No matter how many times the rational part of her brain warned her of the foolishness of this action, her heart had urged her not to wait. She had wrongly accused Rick. She needed to make amends. He had spent a lifetime being judged by other people's standards. He'd been condemned for being a loner, an outsider, a brooding hell-raiser.

Rick flung open the door. Lori Lee jumped back to avoid being knocked sideways. He glared at her, his brown eyes narrowing speculatively.

"What the hell are you doing here?"

She looked at him, all six feet four inches of hard, lean man. Grease streaks smeared his forehead and the edge of his jaw. His ragged jeans and thermal underwear top were stained and dirty. An unruly lock of his long black hair hung over one eye.

She tried to speak, but her vocal cords wouldn't cooperate, issuing only a squeaking sound. She gazed up at him pleadingly. The howling wind whirled dead leaves and scattered debris around Lori Lee's ankles. Shivering, she crossed her arms over her chest and gripped her elbows in an effort to stay warm.

"Come on. Get in here before you freeze to death out there." Rick closed and locked the door behind them, then clasped her shoulder, jerking her around to face him. "What do you want?"

"We need to talk," Lori Lee told him.

"I think you already said just about everything you wanted to say. I don't have time to listen to any more of your parenting lectures." He noticed her looking over his shoulder, surveying the garage's interior and Powell Goodman's disassembled vehicle. "By the way, how did you know where to find me?"

"Eve." She cleared her throat, then lowered the jacket hood from her head and swung her head to free her hair. "Your sister stopped by my house and explained everything to me."

Damn, he wished she wouldn't do that. Swing her hair that way. Lori Lee had the most beautiful hair. It fell below her shoulder blades in thick, blond waves. He'd gotten more than one hard-on wondering what it would be like to have that mass of gold spread out on his pillow as he plunged deeply into her welcoming body.

"So Eve set you straight on a few things, huh? I still don't understand what you're doing here." Releasing her shoulder, he glowered at her. Why hadn't Eve left well enough alone? He never should have told his sister what had happened. He'd had no idea she'd confront Lori Lee.

"I came to apologize," she said.

Rick grunted, then turned his back on her and stomped over to the Corvette. "Go home. Leave me the hell alone."

She instinctively knew that he was more hurt than angry. She had been the one who'd hurt him, and it was up to her to make amends.

"It's not very warm in here," she said, determined to stay and make Rick listen to her. "Isn't there any heat?"

"Kerosene heater." He nodded toward the small round heater near the back of the garage. "It mostly knocks off the chill. The place isn't insulated and what windows aren't broken are cracked."

"I had no idea anyone still used this place for anything." She walked toward him, careful to avoid stepping on the various tools and car parts lying about on the floor. "It should have been condemned and torn down years ago."

"The rent's cheap," he told her. "That's all that's important to me."

"I take it that this—" she pointed to the shell of the vehicle "—is Powell Goodman's '59 'Vette. He told me he was having it restored, but I had no idea you were doing the work. That is, not until Eve explained about—''

"You're dating Powell, aren't you?" Rick jerked a orange rag from his back pocket and wiped the grime off his hands.

"Yes, Powell and I have been seeing each other for a couple of years now."

"Sleeping with him?"

Lori Lee gasped, then wished she hadn't when she saw the smirky grin on Rick's face. "I don't think that's any of your business."

"Are you going to marry him?"

"He's asked me," she said.

"What's keeping you from saying yes?"

For one thing she wasn't in love with Powell. For another, she didn't think he really loved her. Like Tory, Powell thought of her as an asset, someone to impress his friends and associates. She was not only decorative on a man's arm, but she possessed the type of breeding and taste some men thought essential in a mate.

"If Powell were the right man, you'd be willing to risk everything to be his wife."

Lori Lee froze to the spot. Her gaze clashed with Rick's, and she knew he saw the truth in her eyes. She hated being exposed this way. "Powell would make a fine husband for almost any woman," she said. Rick took several steps toward her. "I'm seeing Jimmy Davison, too." Rick moved in on her. "You remember Jimmy, don't you?"

Rick slipped one arm around her waist, then cupped her chin between his thumb and forefinger. "If you really came here to apologize, then I'm listening. And if you want to make it up to me for condemning me unjustly, I know just the way.''

When he lowered his head, intent on kissing her, Lori Lee shoved him away. "No, Rick. I—I did come to apologize, and to tell you that I'd like to be your friend. And Darcie's friend."

Lifting his eyebrows in a skeptical gesture, he stared at her, then broke into hearty laughter. "You want to be my friend?"

"Yes. After Eve explained about your working two jobs and the reason why, I understood and sympathized. If you and Darcie are going to fit in around here, you'll need help I know Eve and Tom will do their part, but I'm in a position to smooth the way, especially for Darcie."

"Why would you want to help me and my daughter?"

Lori Lee wanted to be honest with him without revealing her innermost feelings. If she allowed Rick to see how vulnerable she was to him and to his child, he might well take advantage of her and plunge them all into a situation that could lead only to disappointment and hurt for everyone.

"I admire what you're trying to do," Lori Lee said. "I was wrong to call you an irresponsible parent and to accuse you of...well, of—"

"I believe your exact words were tomcatting around."

"Don't remind me." Reaching out, she clasped Rick's arm. "I'm sorry that I jumped to all the wrong conclusions, that I assumed you were the same old Rick."

He glanced down at her hand circling his forearm. Before she could protest, he grabbed her and pulled her into an intimate embrace. With his face leaning into hers, he whispered against her lips. "I thought you kind of liked the old Rick."

"I was fascinated by you, but I was also afraid of you," she admitted breathlessly.

"How do you feel about me now?" he asked, brushing her lips lightly with his own. "Do you find the new Rick fascinating? Are you still afraid of me?"

"I respect you for wanting to make something of yourself so you can give your child a better life than the one you had." When he laid his cheek against hers, she closed her eyes, savoring the rough, bristly feel of his beard. Rick smelled of grease and sweat and pure masculine power Lori Lee swallowed hard. "And yes, you still fascinate me and still frighten me. You have an effect on me I can't explain.''

"Lori Lee," he groaned her name just as he took her mouth.

Pure pleasure spiraled through her as he kissed her with tender possession. When she didn't resist, he deepened and strengthened his assault. He grabbed her by the back of her head, pressing her into his marauding mouth. She should tell him to stop, but she couldn't. She should tell him that all she had to offer was friendship, but she didn't. She should warn him that they had no future together, but she suspected he already knew.

Lori Lee gave herself over to the moment, to the sweet, glorious feeling of being in Rick's arms, of taking and giving pleasure almost beyond enduring. He always had and always would be forbidden to her. A man not to trust. A temptation to be resisted. But she couldn't resist him, didn't want to resist him, tonight.

"You have no idea how much I want you," he mouthed the words against the pulse throbbing in her neck. "Every time I look at you, I get hard and all I can think about is making love to you."

Her body quivered. Her stomach fluttered. "Rick, please...I didn't come here for this. I came here to..."

But when he kissed her again, she forgot what she was saying, forgot why she was protesting. All she wanted was Rick. Here. Now. Hot and wild and filling her body with his strength.

Caressing her buttocks, he lifted her into his arousal. Standing on tiptoe, she rubbed against him, then ran her fingers up his neck and into his hair. Grabbing his hair, she held his face to hers, and took charge of their kiss, commanding him to return her passionate forcefulness.

Cupping her back end, he lifted her. She wrapped her legs around his hips and draped her arms around his neck. He kissed her, his tongue thrusting into her warm, wet mouth. He carried her toward the old, battered wooden table in the back corner of the garage. Holding her against him with one arm, he reached down and swiped the stack of clean rags and assorted tools off the table. The tools hit the floor with a loud clatter.

Rick sat Lori Lee on the table, then unsnapped and unzipped her jeans. "If you don't want this as much as I do, honey, say so now, 'cause in a couple of seconds I'll be too far gone to stop."

Who was he kidding? He was past that point already. He was in the if-anyone-tries-to-stop-me-I'll-kill-them stage. At this precise moment, nothing mattered except making love to Lori Lee. Here. Now. As soon as humanly possible.

His sex strained painfully against the crotch of his jeans. "I'm in a world of hurt, baby."

Lifting her hips, she pulled her jeans off and tossed them on the floor. She was already beyond reasoning. She acted purely on instincts and feelings. "Don't talk. Don't talk. Just—"

While he kissed her over and over again, he delved his hand inside her bikini panties. He cupped her mound, then stroked her feminine core. She squirmed and moaned and clung to Rick, saying his name repeatedly between heated kisses. He slid two fingers inside her, testing her readiness. She was wet and hot with need.

She cried out. Her body tightened around his fingers. He jerked her panties down and off. She kicked them aside.

He loosened himself from his jeans and boxer shorts, leaned over and plunged into Lori Lee. She clawed his back with her nails, clutched his hips with her knees and bit into his shoulder.

He rode her hard and fast. She met him thrust for thrust, lunge for lunge. Giving and taking, they mated with primitive abandon. He told her how much he wanted her, how wonderful it was to be inside her, how good loving her felt. She begged him to give her all of himself, and he did.

Then almost before it had begun, it ended, the two of them exploding into spasms of release, like a couple of blazing meteorites crashing to earth. They clung to each other, their breaths ragged, sweat coating their bodies, and the aftershocks of pleasure continued rippling through them.

"Oh, Rick, I..." Her chest rose and fell rapidly.

He took her face in his hands and looked deeply into her eyes. "This wasn't the way I wanted our first time to be, honey. I'm sorry, but I couldn't stop."

"Don't blame yourself." She laid her hand on his chest and felt the powerful beat of his heart. "This was as much my fault as yours. I should have stopped you." Suddenly she felt naked and vulnerable. She glanced at her panties and jeans lying on the dirty floor.

Pulling away from her, Rick reached down, picked up her jeans and panties and then helped her put them on. He kissed the side of her neck. "Have I screwed things up so badly that you'll never forgive me?" He zipped up his own jeans.

Standing, she slipped her arm around his waist. "I suppose this was inevitable. We've both wondered about what it would be like if we... Now, we know."

"Yeah. Now we know." *Now we know that we're explosive together, that we go wild in each other's arms, that nothing has ever been this good.*

"I came here to offer you friendship," Lori Lee told him. "I'd like to think we can still be friends, that you'll still allow me to help you and Darcie."

"Is that all you want us to be, Lori Lee, friends?" he asked.

"What do you want?"

"I want *you,* honey. I've always wanted you."

He tried to kiss her, but she pushed him away. "No, I mean what do you want out of life, for you and Darcie?"

"You know what I want," he said. "I want to be sole owner of Bobo's business. I want to marry a good woman and give Darcie the right kind of mother. And someday I'd like to have a couple of more kids. I want my family to be accepted here in Tuscumbia, to be part of this town.''

"I'd like to see you get what you want. I don't know if people will ever totally accept you. It may take years for you to prove to them that you're a changed man.''

"I've got the rest of my life.''

"I'll do whatever I can to help you. We can start by putting what happened tonight behind us and—''

"What the hell's wrong with you?'' he asked. "Are you trying to tell me that I might be good enough for a quickie, but I'm not good enough to marry?''

"No. I...I...''

He closed his eyes momentarily, not wanting to see the regret in her blue eyes. Then he opened them again and looked directly at her, his focused stare challenging her as surely as his words did. "Do you honestly think that this one time got all the lust out of our systems? Don't you know we're going to want to have sex again and again and again?''

"There's no future for us as anything except friends. That's all I can offer you.''

Grabbing her shoulders, he shook her soundly. "Dammit, woman, don't do this to us!''

Tears welled up in her eyes, but she blinked them away. "What happened between us tonight was sex, wasn't it? You just said so. It had nothing to do with love or marriage or forever after. Please, try to understand—''

He flung her away from him. She staggered, almost falling. Standing there with tears clouding her vision and her body trembling, she wished she had the courage to be completely honest with him.

"I understand all right,'' he said. "The apology and the offer of friendship were just excuses, weren't they? You came here wanting to get laid.'' She gasped. He laughed mockingly. "Well, you got what you came for, you can leave now. I've got work to do.''

"Rick, please don't act this way. Don't—''

"Get out!" he demanded, then turned his back on her and pretended to inspect the tools laid out on the floor at his feet.

Quivering from head to toe, her stomach twisted into knots and her weak legs uncooperative, Lori Lee lifted one foot and then the other, forcing herself to walk out of the garage. The moment she opened her car and slid inside, she gripped the steering wheel, lowered her head and cried. Her body shook with sobs as she released the pain and disillusionment in her heart.

What had she expected from a man like Rick Warrick? She was such a fool. She had played with fire and gotten badly burned. From now on, she'd be more careful.

Five

Five

"**I** think it's absolutely sinful for one woman to get so many flowers on Valentine's day." Deanie Webber flitted from arrangement to arrangement, sniffing the roses like a bee collecting pollen. "Five dozen roses! Three dozen red and two dozen pink."

"I thought you stayed after the twirlers' party to help me clean up." Lori Lee gathered up red paper plates, napkins and cups scattered around the studio.

"I did. See. I'm working." Deanie swept cupcake crumbs from the floor into a dustpan. "Tell me, how does it feel to be the most popular single woman in Tuscumbia?"

"At the moment I feel tired. Between preparing for this Valentine's party and getting the girls ready to go to Clanton this weekend, I'm exhausted."

Deanie glanced at her daughter, Katie, and at Darcie Warrick. Both girls sat on the sofa, nibbling candy hearts and comparing Valentine cards they'd received at school today and during the Dixie Twirlers party.

Deanie swept her way over to the wastebasket where Lori Lee was dumping the trash. "I couldn't help but notice that Rick didn't send you any flowers."

"Why should Rick send me flowers?"

"Because he's one of your many admirers, isn't he?"

"I don't know how Rick thinks of me," Lori Lee lied. "I'd like to be his friend, but—"

"His friend?" Deanie rolled her eyes heavenward. "If I were you, I'd want to be more than just friends with him. At the very least, I'd want to be lovers."

"Deanie, will you hush. Little ears hear everything." Lori Lee nodded toward Katie and Darcie.

"They're not paying any attention to us, so don't try to change the subject."

"I have no relationship with Rick. Not now, nor will I have one in the future. He may have changed in a lot of ways, but he's still the type who reaches out and grabs what he wants when he wants it, and—" she lowered her voice to a whisper "—to hell with the consequences."

Manacling Lori Lee's wrist, Deanie pulled her friend to her side. "Something happened between you two, didn't it?"

A pale pink flush covered Lori Lee's cheeks. "Let's just say that Rick Warrick is still a little too crude and rough-edged for me." She jerked her wrist out of Deanie's grasp. "Keep an eye on things for me for a few minutes. I've got to take out the trash."

Lori Lee lifted the plastic bag liner from the wastebasket, pulled the drawstrings and carried it through the storage room and into the alley. She dumped the bag into the garbage bin, then leaned against the brick wall.

The tingling heat of remembrance consumed her, taking her mind and body back to those stolen moments with Rick. Unless he had told someone, only the two of them knew about what had happened at the garage four nights ago. She fervently wished she could forget, but she couldn't. For as long as she lived, she would remember her wild, animalistic coupling with Rick. She'd never known desire so strong, need so powerful, hunger so overwhelming.

Even if Rick told someone, they wouldn't believe him. Everyone knew that Lori Lee Guy was a lady, and by today's standards, a rather old-fashioned lady. People said she was beautiful, talented and intelligent. Men didn't just date her—they courted her. She'd been told, by more than one admirer, that she was the type of woman a man put up on a pedestal and worshiped.

Rick Warrick hadn't courted her, hadn't set her on a pedestal and worshiped her. He had taken her with savage abandon, releasing the untamed part of her that no other man had ever touched. For her, their coupling had been an earth-shattering experience, but she suspected that for him it had been nothing more than one more in a long line of conquests.

Lori Lee couldn't deny the sexual attraction she felt for Rick. But people couldn't build a future together on nothing but sex. She wanted and needed certain things in her life, the things that had always been important to her. She had a place in the social structure, here in Tuscumbia. She was a member of the church where her family had attended services for generations. She belonged to the same clubs that her mother and grandmother had. She dated well-educated, wealthy men who shared her interests. If and when she committed herself to a second marriage, she would fall in love with one of her own kind, a man to whom marriage would mean a lifetime commitment.

A frigid evening wind tousled her hair. Shivering, Lori Lee rubbed her hands together, then rushed into the storage room. The sound of girlish giggles drifted on the air. The party had ended twenty minutes ago, but Rick hadn't picked up his daughter. Had he overslept again?

She hadn't seen him since the night they'd made love—if you could call what they'd done together making love.

And she didn't want to see him again. She wasn't ready to face him after what had happened.

Dear God, she'd been a fool to give herself to him the way she had. How many other women had been seduced by his raw, compelling masculinity? Even if other barriers didn't stand between them, Rick's womanizing ways would.

Just as she'd done every day since their last encounter, Lori Lee mentally listed all the reasons she and Rick could never make a relationship work. They were from different worlds, with different backgrounds and different friends. Her social set would never accept him. He was a ladies' man, with an earthy sex appeal that drew women to him like moths to a flame. He probably hadn't ever been faithful to a woman in his life. How could she believe he'd be faithful to her?

If Lori Lee were truly honest with herself, she'd have to admit that she really didn't care what anyone thought about Rick. She was no longer a teenage girl, restrained by society's rules and afraid to take a chance on loving the town bad boy. She was a woman now, a woman not concerned with Rick Warrick's social standing, but a woman worried about being hurt again, of having the man she loved be unfaithful to her.

But the biggest barrier between them—between her and any man who wanted children—was her infertility. If and when Rick remarried, he wanted more children. She couldn't have a child of her own, and she suspected a macho guy like Rick wouldn't want to raise kids that weren't his.

"Hey, Lori Lee," Deanie called out from the studio. "I've got to run. Want me to take Darcie home?"

"No, that's okay." Lori Lee plastered a phony smile on her face and walked into the studio. "If Rick doesn't show up in a few minutes, I'll drop Darcie by Eve's on my way home."

"You won't have to do that," Darcie said, peering out

the glass door. "I see Daddy's truck. He's just pulling into a parking place out front."

"Don't forget to ask him if you can spend the night with me sometime soon," Katie said.

Lori Lee held Darcie's jacket while the child slipped her arms into the sleeves. "I'll ask him," Darcie promised, then looked up at Lori Lee. "I told my daddy that I want him to go to Clanton with us Saturday for the competition, and he's promised me he'll go."

"That's wonderful, Darcie." Lori Lee zipped up the little girl's jacket and lifted the attached hood over her head. "He's going to be so proud of you when he sees you perform."

Rick held the door open for Deanie and her daughter with one hand, while clutching a single yellow rose behind his back. Deanie smiled and spoke. Lori Lee's best friend was always cordial and friendly. He wished the other members of her social circle were half as nice.

He'd thought about asking Eve to pick up Darcie today, but decided he couldn't put off facing Lori Lee any longer. Four nights ago, she had left the garage angry and hurt. He had handled the situation all wrong. God, he'd been an idiot to take her the way he had. Lori Lee was no good-time girl. She was a lady. An angel. A dream. And he was as unworthy of her as a man could be.

He had wanted her for such a long time. And when she'd finally given herself to him, what had he done? He'd taken her with all the finesse of a rutting bull! She had told him that what had happened between them had nothing to do with love or marriage or forever after. Maybe she was right. Hell, he didn't know. Maybe it had been lust and nothing more. He'd never truly loved a woman, and wasn't sure what to call the way he felt about Lori Lee. Lust? Definitely. Obsession? Maybe. But love? He didn't know.

What he did know was that, after thinking things over, he'd decided the one thing he knew he *did* want from Lori Lee Guy was friendship. If her offer to help Darcie was sincere, he'd be crazy to refuse. Despite his feelings for Lori Lee—whatever they were—his main concern had to be his child. If he didn't take care of her, give her a good life, then he would have failed at what mattered most to him.

He didn't want his little girl ever to suffer the way he had. He'd always been on the outside looking in. It wasn't going to be that way for Darcie!

And if he had a prayer of building any kind of relationship with Lori Lee, he'd have to change his tactics. Whether the end result would be a friendship or a love affair, only time would tell. But he had to go about this slow and easy. Instead of taking what he wanted from her, he had to wait until she was willing to give. So willing that there would be no regrets later.

Rick closed the door behind him, shutting out the cold February evening. He glanced across the room to where Lori Lee was tying the strings on Darcie's hood into a bow. He closed his eyes at the sight of the beautiful golden woman and the child who was her very image.

Before returning to Tuscumbia, he had marveled at his daughter's resemblance to Lori Lee. But since it had been so many years since he'd seen Lori Lee, he thought he might have imagined how much Darcie looked like her. But seeing the two together was a true revelation.

April had been a blue-eyed blonde. He'd been attracted to her because she reminded him of Lori Lee. But for some odd reason, Darcie looked more like Lori Lee than she did her own mother. Or maybe he saw only what he wanted to see.

Lori Lee Guy represented everything Rick had ever wanted. If Darcie could be like Lori Lee, then it was reasonable to assume she could live Lori Lee's storybook life.

"Daddy!" Darcie ran to her father and grabbed his hand. "Come say hello to Lori Lee. I've been telling her that you can go with us to Clanton this Saturday."

Rick glanced hesitantly at Lori Lee while he held Darcie's hand and kept the single rose hidden behind his back.

"Hello, Rick."

Seeing him again was more difficult than she'd thought it would be. He was so incredibly, tantalizingly male. Her nipples tightened; her body moistened. He'd been right when he said having sex once wouldn't be enough for either of them.

Rick knew it wasn't going to be easy seeing Lori Lee again. He just hadn't realized it would be this difficult. Why did she have to be so damn beautiful? Just looking at her turned him on. She was the stuff of male fantasies. Large breasts, long legs, sultry lips and a mane of blond curls. Her red leather, calf-length skirt had a side slit that revealed one shapely thigh. A soft, beige cashmere sweater hugged her lush figure and a gold locket rested between her breasts.

"Sorry I'm late," he said. "I had an errand to run that took longer than I expected." At the last minute, he'd decided to stop by the florist shop and get a rose for Lori Lee—a combination peace offering and Valentine gift. He wished that he could have bought her a dozen, but they were too expensive, so he'd bought the one yellow rose. Yellow roses always reminded him of Lori Lee—all sunshine, bright and golden as springtime.

"No problem." Lori Lee had thought she could see Rick again without succumbing to his potent charisma. She'd been wrong. Just looking at him made her want him. It wasn't just one thing that made him so irresistible, but a combination. His big, hard body. His devilish smile. His penetrating brown eyes. His lips. His hands. His— "Uh, er, I'm glad you'll get to go to Clanton with us, especially since this will be Darcie's first competition. I'm amazed at how quickly she learns. She seems to have a natural talent for performing."

"I'm looking forward to going," he said.

"Good." Think of something to say, she told herself. Don't just stand here acting like a fool. "Uh, would you like a cupcake and some punch? There's plenty left over from the party.''

"No, thanks." He glanced around the studio, noticing how Lori Lee had decorated for Valentine's Day. Big red hearts and cupids covered the walls, along with a variety of Valentine cards. Red and white streamers hung from the ceiling. And dozens of red and pink roses decorated Lori Lee's desk as well as the coffee and end tables.

"Isn't everything pretty?" Darcie said. "Lori Lee makes everything fun." She tugged on her father's hand. "Come look at the beautiful flowers all of Lori Lee's boyfriends sent her. Katie's mommy said that Lori Lee's the most popular girl in Tuscumbia."

"Yeah, she always was," Rick said.

So the roses were from Lori Lee's many admirers, huh? The guys she dated could afford to send her flowers by the dozens. If he gave her his one puny little rose, she'd probably laugh in his face. Who was he kidding, thinking he could compete with men like Powell Goodman and Jimmy Davison? They could offer her everything. What could he offer her? Nothing but himself and another woman's child. Why on earth would she want either?

"We've got to go, sweetie," Rick told Darcie. "I'm taking my best girl to McDonald's for hamburgers. Remember?"

"I haven't forgotten," Darcie said, then looked at Lori Lee. "I wish you could go with us, but I suppose you've already got a date."

Rick opened his mouth to speak, to somehow find a way to take back his daughter's invitation, but Lori Lee responded first. "Yes, I do have a date. Mr. Davison and I have reservations at Dale's for dinner."

"Good night, then," Rick said. "We'll meet you here Saturday morning bright and early."

Lori Lee watched Rick and Darcie as they left the studio. Just before helping his daughter up into the truck, Rick dropped something on the ground. With her heart thumping loudly in her ears, Lori Lee hurried across the room and looked out the front door. There on the sidewalk in front of Rick's battered pickup truck lay a single yellow rose. She waited until he pulled out of the parking place and drove off up Main Street, then she rushed outside and picked up the flower. Clutching it to her breast, she walked slowly back toward the studio. Standing under the awning, she lifted the rose to her lips and stood there watching as the red taillights of Rick's truck disappeared in the darkness.

She had never expected Rick to do something as sentimental and romantic as bring her a single rose for Valentine's Day. Somehow, it didn't fit the image she had of the former bad boy.

Her studio was filled with dozens of perfect red and pink roses, all gifts from men who could easily afford them, men whose secretaries had no doubt ordered them.

Rick Warrick had brought her a single yellow rose—her favorite flower. How had he known?

And why, oh, why, did his gesture mean so much to her if the man meant nothing?

Cursing under his breath, Rick slammed the truck's hood, then kicked the front tire. Damned worthless piece of garbage. If he could afford a decent vehicle, he wouldn't be in this situation.

Darcie rolled down the window, stuck her head out and asked, "What's the matter, Daddy?"

"Looks like I'm stuck here, sweetie." Rick tried to calm the anger in his voice. "The radiator has sprung a leak. It'll take about three hours for me to take it off, get it repaired and put it back on. I'm sorry, Darcie, but you'll have to ride with Lori Lee. I'll drive down later."

Lori Lee had just told the caravan of parents and Dixie Twirlers to head on out, that she would follow them shortly. On these trips, they tried to travel as a group, in case anyone had car trouble.

"What's the problem?" Lori Lee asked Rick as she pulled her car to a stop beside the truck.

"Daddy's radiator's got a leak and he says I should ride with you," Darcie said.

"I hope you don't mind taking her with you." Rick opened the truck door and lifted Darcie down onto the sidewalk. "I'll get her stuff."

"I don't mind taking her." Lori Lee adored Darcie, and that was the problem. Several of the twirler mothers had mentioned how attached Lori Lee was to the child, and Mara Royce had even accused her of playing favorites. Despite the circumstances, her allowing Darcie to ride to Clanton with her was bound to create some jealous feelings.

"I should be able to get the truck fixed and be on the road behind y'all in a couple of hours at most." Rick ruffled Darcie's long, blond curls. "I can't miss my best girl's first performance, can I?"

"If you don't mind leaving the truck here, you're welcome to ride with me, too. That way, you won't miss anything." The moment she issued the invitation, Lori Lee wished she could take it back. Dear Lord, if some of the parents would object to her chauffeuring Darcie to and from Clanton, what would they say about Rick riding with her?

"Yes, Daddy. Please. Leave your truck. You can fix it tomorrow." Darcie looked up at her father pleadingly and he knew he could refuse her nothing.

"Are you sure you don't mind?" he asked.

Lori Lee pushed the automatic release button and opened her trunk. "Put Darcie's things in the trunk and hurry. We need to get going."

Rick's gut instincts warned him that he was making a mistake, but what the hell. It wasn't every day he and Darcie would get to spend several hours alone with Lori Lee. He wasn't sure who was happier at the prospect, he or his daughter.

During the competition, Rick felt uncomfortable sitting with the other parents. Several had made it perfectly clear he was an unwelcome intrusion. Everyone else simply ignored him, everyone except Deanie Webber and her husband, Phil, who not only spoke to him but invited him to sit with them.

One twirler mother, a divorcée whose name he couldn't remember, kept flirting with him, and when he continued to ignore her, she'd moved over and sat by him. More than once, he overheard Mara Royce make comments about the fact he and Darcie had ridden to Clanton with Lori Lee, and wondered if something was going on there, or if not, then was he fooling around with Sherry's mother?

Finally Deanie Webber took pity on him and came to his rescue when she overheard the flirtatious brunette at his side proposition him. She not only got rid of his unwanted admirer, she gave Mara Royce something else to think about besides Lori Lee and him.

"Hon, Mara needs to speak to you," Deanie told the woman. "She wants your opinion on a routine she plans to suggest to Lori Lee. Of course, I said your little Sherry should have the lead part, but she wants Steffie—"

"Catch you later, handsome," Sherry's mother said as she jumped up and made her way up the bleachers.

"Thanks," Rick said. "I thought she was going to crawl in my lap any minute now."

Deanie laughed. Rick liked the way she laughed. Full-bodied and genuine. "Someone should have warned you about Bitsy. And as for these other yokels, don't let them bother you. Given time, most of the folks will come around. They just don't know quite what to think of you."

"Yeah, I suppose you're right. A lot of them remember me from school, and the others have heard about my hoodlum days."

"I think you should know that Mara Royce is none too happy that Lori Lee is so taken with Darcie." Deanie placed her hand on Rick's arm. "Darcie is a beautiful child, and very talented. But Mara doesn't see it that way. She's going to assume that Darcie's being given special treatment for some personal reason.''

''Are you saying that Mrs. Royce can cause trouble for Lori Lee?'' Rick asked.

''Mara thinks her Steffie should be the center of the world, and anything or anyone that gets in the way of that is in danger from Mara.''

''She sounds like a real bitch to me, and her kid has to be a spoiled brat.''

''Right on both counts,'' Deanie said. ''But don't be surprised at anything Mara says or does.''

''Yeah. Thanks for letting me know who my enemies are.''

When the competition ended, the Dixie Twirlers had captured first place in several events, including Twinkle Toe's Halftime Show Dance Line. All the girls were giddy with success; most parents were proud and happy.

While Lori Lee gave the girls an after-competition pep talk inside the gym, the parents loaded all the twirlers' paraphernalia into their vehicles. A light cold drizzle had begun falling, and the night air was frigid.

Just as Rick opened Lori Lee's trunk, he heard someone approach him. Turning around, he saw Dr. Eugene Royce, a bald, heavyset, fortyish man staring at him.

''Yeah?'' Rick noticed Mara Royce standing several yards away, watching her husband.

''I, er, that is, we thought someone should speak to you about Lori Lee.'' Eugene cleared his throat. ''We're very fond of her. Think the world of her. She's a fine woman.''

''I agree.'' Rick placed the twirler equipment in the trunk and closed the lid.

''I'm glad you know the kind of person Lori Lee is,'' Eugene said. ''I'm sure you didn't intend to, er, that is…we don't want you to get the wrong idea.''

''The wrong idea about what?'' Rick asked, towering over Eugene a good five inches. ''The wrong idea about

Lori Lee? Or the wrong idea about why you're trying to warn me to stay away from her?''

"We're not warning you, just advising you." Gazing into Rick's eyes, Eugene took a step backward. "Surely you realize how unsuitable you are for Lori Lee. She's not your kind."

"And what is my kind?"

"Well, someone, er, that is, someone less—"

Rick stepped forward, glowering at the other man. "Tell your wife that there is absolutely nothing going on between Lori Lee Guy and me. Ms. Guy has been kind to me and my daughter, out of the goodness of her heart." Rick grabbed Eugene's shoulder, clutching tightly. "And if anyone starts spreading any lies about Ms. Guy, I won't like it."

Forty-six girls, ranging in age from three to fourteen, raced out of the gymnasium, squealing when they felt the icy sleet peppering down on them.

Deanie Webber rushed toward Lori Lee. "Get over there, quick." She pointed toward the parking lot where Rick stood gripping Eugene Royce's shoulder. "I don't know what's going on, but Rick looks awfully upset, and Mara is standing over there glaring a hole in him."

"Oh, damn!" Lori Lee said. "Keep Darcie with you and Phil until I find out what's going on."

Lori Lee ran over to her car, halting at Rick's side. "Hey, we'd better get going before the roads ice over. We've got a three-hour drive ahead of us."

Rick gave Eugene's shoulder a hard squeeze. "Glad we had this little talk, Dr. Royce. Just remember what I told you." Releasing the other man's shoulder, Rick turned to Lori Lee. "Where's Darcie?"

Eugene scurried off toward his wife, whose sharp, angry voice was masked by the sound of clinking sleet hitting the parking lot pavement.

"She's with Deanie," Lori Lee said. "What was going on here? You looked like you wanted to hit Eugene."

"If I thought that bitch of a wife of his would feel the blow, I'd have hit him." Rick snorted. "She sent him over here honestly thinking he would intimidate me."

Grinning, Lori Lee lifted the hood of her coat over her head. "Eugene is a wealthy, respected orthodontist and he and Mara are social royalty around here. There are a lot of people who are very intimidated by Eugene and Mara's social standing."

Seeing the humor in the situation, Rick laughed, then grabbed Lori Lee by the arm. "You get in the car, honey, out of this sleet. I'll go get Darcie." He unlocked the car with the remote, then opened the door and assisted Lori Lee inside. "How about letting me drive home? I'm sure you're a good driver, but with the weather like it is, I'd—"

"You drive," she told him. "Now, get Darcie and let's head for the Shoals."

By the time they were a few miles outside of Birmingham, Lori Lee realized they were dealing with more than a little rain mixed with sleet. Trees and power lines were icing over and the highway was getting slick. The radio stations announced that an unexpected winter storm had hit North Alabama. Interstate 65 was closed north of Cullman and most state highways were impassable.

Deanie called Lori Lee from her cellular phone and they discussed the situation, agreeing that the Dixie Twirlers and their parents would have no choice but to spend the night in Cullman.

Unfortunately the twirlers from the Shoals area weren't the only stranded travelers seeking refuge. As they drove from motel to motel, the twirlers' caravan began to split up, taking rooms wherever they could find them. When Rick asked at the front desk of the Comfort Lodge, he was told they had one room left, so, without consulting Lori Lee, he handed the desk clerk his credit card and registered them as Mr. and Mrs. Warrick.

When he returned to the car, he found Darcie asleep in Lori Lee's lap, her little head resting on Lori Lee's breast.

He opened the passenger door and said, "I got us a room." He lifted Darcie into his arms. She roused briefly, smiled at her father, then curled up against his chest.

While they walked down the motel corridor, Rick noticed Lori Lee glancing at the single key he held in his hand.

"They just had one room left," he told her. "I figured we'd better take it. I know it'll be kind of awkward, but it's the best I could do."

"None of the other twirler parents are staying here, so no one will know," she said.

"Yeah, no one will know."

He unlocked the door to their room, flipped on the light switch and carried Darcie over to the nearest double bed. Lori Lee rushed ahead of him and turned down the covers. When he laid Darcie down, Lori Lee sat on the bed beside her and removed the child's shoes and jacket.

"She's worn out." Lori Lee pulled the sheet and blanket over the child, then caressed her plump, rosy cheek. "I was so proud of her today. She did the routine perfectly. Better than some of the girls who've had much more practice."

Darcie's eyelids fluttered. She opened her eyes and looked up at the two adults hovering over her. "Hi, Daddy. Hi, Lori Lee."

"Hello, sweetheart." Lori Lee playfully flipped the end of Darcie's nose with her index finger.

"Did Daddy get us a room?"

"He certainly did."

Darcie yawned. "I'm hungry."

"I noticed some vending machines down the hall," Rick said. "You ladies get comfortable and I'll go see what I can round up for us."

"Look in my purse and get some money," Lori Lee said. "I think I've got plenty of quarters and dollar bills."

"If I need your money, I'll come back and get it." Rick opened the door. "Lock up until I get back."

After securing the door, Lori Lee removed her coat and hung it on a rack in the closet. If anyone had told her when she left Tuscumbia this morning that she'd be spending the night in a Cullman motel with Rick Warrick, she'd have told them they were crazy.

Well, crazy or not, here she was. Of course, there was no way anyone could find out that she had shared a room with Rick, and besides, the two of them were hardly alone. Darcie was their chaperone.

She glanced at Rick's daughter, who had closed her eyes and fallen back to sleep. Lori Lee smiled, her heart warmed by Darcie's sweet presence.

Ten minutes later, Lori Lee opened the door when Rick knocked. He balanced two cups of coffee, a carton of milk and three sandwiches in his hands. Packs of cookies and assorted pastries stuck out of his jacket pockets.

"Shh..." Lori Lee removed the sandwiches from the top of the drinks. "She went back to sleep almost immediately."

"Today was a big day for her," he said. "She was so excited, she didn't sleep hardly any last night and she got me up before daylight this morning."

"She may wake up later starving to death." Lori Lee placed the sandwiches on the dresser, then reached out and took the cups, one at a time, and set them down.

Rick emptied his pockets, then removed his coat, tossing it on the lone chair in the room. "I hope you can drink your coffee black. I couldn't find any sweetener or creamer. If you want, you can use some of Darcie's milk."

"Black will be fine." She removed the lid from one of the foam cups, sat on the edge of the bed and sipped the coffee.

Lori Lee and Rick ate their sandwiches in relative silence, each occasionally glancing over at Darcie. The child had curled into a fetal position, with her body facing the wall.

Lori Lee picked up their trash and threw it into the wastebasket, then excused herself. While she was gone, Rick removed his shoes and unbuttoned his shirt. He supposed he had no choice but to sleep in his clothes. Of course, he doubted he'd get much sleep. Not with Lori Lee lying in the bed next to his.

She emerged from the bathroom, her face scrubbed clean of makeup and her hair brushed free and hanging in soft waves down her back.

"I'll sleep with Darcie," she offered. "As big as you are, you might be more comfortable in a bed by yourself."

"Thanks." He surveyed Lori Lee from head to toe, sizing up every curvaceous inch of her lush body. If his daughter wasn't asleep in the room with them— *Dammit, man, don't even think it! Get your mind on something else. You'll spend the whole night hard and hurting if you let yourself think about making love to Lori Lee again.*

He watched her take off her shoes and crawl under the blanket beside Darcie. After removing his boots, he turned down the covers on the other bed, got in and flipped off the table lamp. He lay there unmoving for a while, trying to think of anything except Lori Lee.

After mulling over repairing his truck, figuring out how much money he'd have to borrow to buy out Bobo's part of the business and wondering what kind of season the Braves would have that year, Rick could still hear Lori Lee tossing and turning. Was she having as difficult a time as he was going to sleep? Was she lying over there doing her damnedest not to think about him? Was she remembering what it had been like when they'd made love?

His sex grew hard and heavy. He groaned silently, cursing himself for a fool. Maybe he should put on his coat and boots and run around outside in the sleet until he cooled off. He tossed back the covers, sat up and threw his legs over the side of the bed, facing the window. Spearing his fingers through his hair, he scratched his head and stood.

"Rick?" Lori Lee whispered his name.

"Sorry I disturbed you," he said softly. "I can't sleep. Thought I'd get up for a while."

Drawing back the curtains, he stared out at the empty swimming pool, the edge of the crowded parking area and then up at the black night sky. In the stillness, he listened to the howling wind and the frigid sleet as it hit the icy ground.

He heard the other bed creak and knew Lori Lee was getting up. He stood by the window. Unmoving. Holding his breath. She walked up behind him and laid her hand on his back. He sucked in a deep breath, then let it out slowly.

"I can't sleep, either," she said, then rested her forehead on his shoulder.

Rick eased his arm around her, drawing her close to his side. "You know what I want, don't you?"

"Yes." She melted against him as she put her arms around his waist and laid her head on his chest. "I was a fool to offer you my friendship when we both want..." She lifted her head and looked up in the darkness, barely able to see his strong, chiseled features. "After tonight, we have to stay away from each other."

"Don't ask me to stay away from you," he said. She was asking him to make the ultimate sacrifice, to give her up when he knew she was his for the taking.

"I'll do everything I can to help Darcie. I promise. She's become very special to me. I—I—"

Rick kissed her forehead. She shivered. Caressing her through her slacks, he cupped her hip in his big hand. "What are you so afraid of?" he asked. "I know I'm not good enough for you, that a woman like you would never marry a man like me. But I'm not asking you to marry me, am I? What would be so wrong with the two of us having an affair? We could be discreet. We could find a way to keep it a secret."

She clung to him, tempted by what he was offering, but she knew, even if he didn't, that she simply wasn't the type to have an illicit affair. She didn't have the courage to openly date Rick, despite how desperately she wanted him. She could not take the chance of getting her heart broken and her reputation ruined for a man who wanted only an affair.

"I can't become your lover," she said. "I can't risk everything for a few stolen moments here and there."

"I'd ask you to marry me if I thought—" He took her face in his hands and forced her mouth against his, kissing her possessively. Breaking the kiss, he breathed deeply, gulping in air. "Forget I said that. Why would you marry me, a blue-collar guy with grease under his fingernails and a ready-made family, when you could marry Powell Goodman and have everything money can buy and kids of your own?"

Fighting her body's need to cling to Rick, to wrap around him and find release, Lori Lee somehow managed to stay sane and rational. "If and when I marry again, I'll love my husband deeply and completely and he'll love me the same way."

"Yeah, you'd want love, wouldn't you?"

"Yes, I want love. Don't you?"

"I'd settle for less," he admitted. "If I could find a good, decent woman who wanted to be Darcie's mother, I'd marry her, if the chemistry between us was right."

"You'd want sex whether or not there was any love involved." She had known Rick was a virile man, a man who wanted and needed sex on a regular basis. He wanted her right now, and if Darcie wasn't in the room with them, he would take her to bed and make love to her all night.

And she'd let him.

And he knew it.

"I'd better go back to bed," she said.

He rubbed himself intimately against her, letting her feel his arousal. Closing her eyes, she sighed and gave herself over to one more kiss, a kiss that soon raged out of control. With their bodies glued together, their mouths devouring, their hands groping, Rick walked Lori Lee backward until her legs brushed the edge of the bed. He shoved her onto the bed, then came down on top of her.

He nestled himself between her legs, longing to strip away her clothing and bury himself deep inside her.

"Rick? Rick, we can't do this," she whispered breathlessly.

"I know, dammit!" He jumped up off her, felt around on the floor for his boots and slipped into them. "I'm going for a walk. Lock the door and go to sleep."

Lori Lee sat on the edge of the bed. "You can't go out in weather like this."

"I'll walk around in the hall for a while and then sleep in the lobby."

She started to protest, but realized he was doing what was best for both of them. If he stayed here, neither of them would get any sleep unless they made love. And they couldn't have sex with Rick's daughter asleep in the room with them.

"When we get home, we can't—" she said.

"Don't worry, honey. I'll leave you alone. I won't have any trouble finding myself a more willing woman." He grabbed his coat, opened the door and left.

Lori Lee closed and locked the door, then went into the bathroom and had herself a nice long cry. Get it out of your system now, she told herself. Rick Warrick is still the same heartbreaker he always was. He wants you, but if he can't have you, he'll just get himself another woman. That's exactly what he'd done fifteen years ago, and that's still what he'd do. You were nothing more to him than any other willing woman back then, and that's all you are to him now. Nothing between them had changed. Beneath his reformed facade, Rick was still bad to the bone.

Six

Lori Lee hit the rewind button on her tape player. She had accidently recorded the wrong music for the third performance of the annual recital and would have to record the correct tune over it. She changed the tapes, putting in *Thunder Drums*. The Dixie Darlings, her oldest group, would perform their dance-twirl competition to the hot, wild beat of Scott Fitzgerald's percussive coup de grace. She wanted to make a few changes in the routine before the girls performed the number at the April recital.

Picking up her baton, Lori Lee stood and walked to the center of the room in the downstairs studio. Playing around with her baton, she danced it through her fingers, then tossed it into the air and caught it easily. Taking a second baton from the wall display, she began figuring out the subtle changes she wanted to make in the routine, little things that would make the performance a bit more showy.

Talented performers were essential, but she had discovered that competition judges were often influenced by a group's showmanship. Presentation and ability in equal parts was a winning combination.

Although the recital was still a month away, she wanted to get her plans precisely right today. The girls would need as much extra time as possible for practice.

She'd already begun evaluating each student for the awards Dixie Twirlers presented each year after the final recital performance. She tried to make sure that every student received a small trophy because she didn't want any child to feel left out on the big night. Of course, there were several awards that every child and parent coveted, an important one being Best First-Year Student. She had no doubts about who deserved that trophy. Darcie Warrick. In the two and a half months she'd been with the twirlers, she had shown an aptitude for twirling and performing that was nothing short of amazing.

After her regular class, Lori Lee had taken extra time with Darcie. Ordinarily she charged students for private lessons, but she knew Rick could barely afford what he was already paying. She worried about how he'd pay for the expensive costumes for the recital and upcoming competitions. Knowing what a financial burden Rick was under, Lori Lee had told Aunt Birdie to sell him Darcie's costumes at cost and, if need be, arrange for him to pay for them on credit.

In the month since the Clanton competition and their forced stay at the Cullman motel, Lori Lee and Rick had kept their distance, seeing each other only occasionally. When Rick picked up Darcie from lessons. When they both attended a Deshler basketball game, she with Powell Goodman and he with a woman named Angie Clemmons. Then again when the twirlers had gone to competition at Wetumpka last week. Rick hadn't brought Angie with him, and Lori Lee had been thankful.

She told herself that she didn't care if Rick was dating someone, and certainly didn't care who the woman was. But she had listened when Aunt Birdie and Deanie shared all the local gossip about the woman in Rick's life. Angie Clemmons was a divorcée with an eight-year-old son. She wasn't a local girl, having been born and raised in Georgia. She had moved to town with her former husband four years ago. She worked as a clerk at the local Wal-Mart, and had recently ended a yearlong affair with a coworker, who just happened to be married.

Word was that Angie had a reputation that suited her dark, sultry appearance. It was a well-known fact she liked to spend her time at the Watering Hole, a favorite night spot for adults on the prowl. A friend of a friend of a friend had told Phil Webber that Angie was a wild woman in bed.

One of Lori Lee's batons hit the floor, bounced a couple of times, then rolled to a standstill. Damn! She never dropped a baton. Except when she lost her concentration by allowing her thoughts to wander. She tried not to think about Rick and Angie Clemmons having sex, but the unwanted vision of the two in the throes of passion had caused Lori Lee more than one sleepless night.

Her good sense told her she was doing the smart thing, the only logical thing she could do—keeping away from a man who could cause her nothing but heartache. But her body longed for Rick. For his demanding mouth. His caressing hands. For the earthy words he whispered to her. And for the pleasure of his total possession.

She could lie to Aunt Birdie and to Deanie, and sometimes even to herself. She could deny, a thousand times over, that Rick meant something to her, but in her heart she knew the truth. She wanted Rick so much that she ached with the wanting. And it tore her apart inside to see him with Angie, knowing the two were lovers.

Standing outside the studio, Rick watched Lori Lee while she performed with two batons. Even through the closed door he could hear the powerful beat of the primitive music. She danced to the rhythm, her graceful body smoothly executing the complicated movements. This was the girl he remembered from high school, the beauty queen who took his breath away every time he looked at her. But she was a woman now, more beautiful in maturity, her body ripened with lush curves. The hot-pink tights and black leotards she wore clung to her body like a second skin, revealing the perfection of her feminine form.

His sex grew heavy. He cursed under his breath. He was no horny teenager, but his reaction to her certainly made him feel like one. Why was it that no other woman could appease his hunger for Lori Lee?

He had stayed away from her for more than a month now, but he hadn't stopped thinking about her or wanting her. He had hoped dating Angie Clemmons would help ease the gnawing ache inside him. But it hadn't. Angie was more than willing. Hell, she was eager. But Angie wasn't the woman he wanted.

He dreaded going into the studio and confronting Lori Lee, but his pride demanded a showdown. He hadn't liked the idea of Lori Lee giving Darcie special lessons, free of charge, but because her time with Lori Lee meant so much to Darcie, he'd swallowed his pride and kept his mouth shut. But what had just happened a few minutes ago was more than his pride could stand.

He'd taken his lunch break to stop by the Sparkle and Shine shop and check on buying Darcie's costumes for the upcoming recital. She'd brought home the list of outfits she would need, the prices printed beside each item. The cost had been staggering for a guy who didn't have an extra dollar to his name, but he'd made arrangements with Tom and Eve to spend his free Saturdays during the next few weeks painting their house. The advance they'd given him would cover Darcie's costumes, with enough left over to pay for whatever twirler stuff she'd need during the spring and summer.

When he'd gone to pay Aunt Birdie for the recital costumes, she had quoted him a price far below what had been printed on the list Darcie had brought home. He had mentioned the price list to Aunt Birdie, who'd turned beet red, then hemmed and hawed, and tried to convince him that the prices on the list had been inaccurate. But Rick knew better, and when he pressed Aunt Birdie for the truth, she'd admitted Lori Lee had asked her to sell him the costumes at cost.

What the hell did she think he was, a charity case? He hadn't taken charity from anybody since he'd left his last foster home and joined the army. A. K. Warrick paid his own way, and he was going to make damn sure that Lori Lee Guy didn't make the mistake of feeling sorry for him ever again.

Rick swung open the studio door. Lori Lee immediately stopped dancing. Tilting her head to see who had entered, she opened her mouth on a silent gasp.

"We need to talk." He slammed the door behind him and marched into the studio.

Clasping a baton in each hand, Lori Lee stood ramrod straight as Rick approached her. His thick, sensuous lips were set in a hard frown. He glowered at her with eyes narrowed into slits. His big hands were clutched into tight fists at his sides. He looked as if he had come to do battle, and she was his enemy.

"Is something wrong?" she asked, determined to show no fear, although the sight of Rick in such a rage unnerved her.

"Yes, there's something wrong," he said. "Something bad wrong."

"Darcie? Is she all right? Nothing's happened to—"

"Darcie's fine." His voice softened slightly when he spoke his daughter's name.

"You're obviously very upset. Are you angry with me about something?" She fidgeted with the batons she held, unconsciously waltzing them through her fingers.

"Yeah, you could say that." Glaring down at her nervous hands, he reached out and grabbed her wrists, stopping her agitated movements.

She jerked away from his hold, turned and laid the batons on her desk. With unsteady legs and quivering stomach she turned to face him. "Well?"

"I don't want your damn charity. I can pay for Darcie's costumes without any discounts from you!"

"Oh." A rosy blush stained her cheeks.

"Yeah, oh. Did you think I don't have sense enough to figure out something's rotten when the price Aunt Birdie quoted me for Darcie's costumes was a lot less than on the price list you sent home?"

She'd given the price list to the parents when they picked up their children. She hadn't sent one to Rick. How had Darcie gotten one? "Oh, she wasn't supposed to—"

"Don't think I'm not grateful for all the extra time you give Darcie." Taking a deep breath, Rick stuffed his hands into his front pockets and pivoted slightly back on his heels. "She's really blossomed since she started taking lessons from you. You're all she talks about. Lori Lee says this. Lori Lee does that. I get a dose of Lori Lee every morning with breakfast and every evening with supper."

"I'm sorry if—"

"No, I'm not complaining." How could he find fault with his daughter's choice of a role model, when the woman she'd chosen was the woman he had idolized for as long as he could remember? "I can't think of anyone I'd rather Darcie emulate than you. You're the kind of woman I want my daughter to become."

"I'm very fond of Darcie. She's a wonderful child." *I wish she were mine. It's almost sinful the way I've come to adore her.*

"Look, I... Keep on being Darcie's friend. She needs you." Shutting his eyes momentarily, Rick clenched his jaw and took another deep breath, then opened his eyes and looked Lori Lee squarely in the face. "Don't ever try to play the benevolent benefactress with me again. I don't have much, not when it comes to money or social position, but I do have my pride. I work for what I want. Do you understand? I don't take charity from anybody, but especially not from you."

"I'm sorry if I offended you, but I know how difficult things are for you right now. I just thought—"

He grabbed her shoulders; she stiffened at his touch. A charge of pure electrical energy passed between them, surging through their bodies, making each acutely aware of the other. Their gazes met and locked. Lori Lee shivered.

"Damn you! And damn me, too." He growled the words, his voice a coarse, deadly whisper.

"Rick?"

He shouldn't have touched her. Hell, he shouldn't have come here and confronted her. When would he ever learn that with Lori Lee he couldn't control the situation?

"Tell me that you don't want me," he said. "Tell me that I've done the right thing staying away from you."

"Yes, you've done the right thing. You've done what was best for both of us."

When he stroked her cheek with his fingertip, she closed her eyes and sighed. She had to move away from him. She couldn't allow anything to happen between them. Not now, not here, at her studio with a glass front open onto Main Street.

"Please don't, Rick," she pleaded with him.

Releasing her, he let his hands drop to his sides. "It would make things easier for me if you told me you didn't want me. Whenever I'm this close to you, my body tells me that you're mine. Tell me you're not."

"I'm not yours," she said hurriedly, forcing the words. "You don't need me. Remember, you have Angie Clemmons now."

He grunted derisively. "Yeah, I've got Angie, and you've got Powell Goodman, haven't you? Aren't we a couple of lucky people. You've got a rich, respected blue blood panting after you, and I've got a hot, sexy little brunette who can't get enough of me. What more could either of us want?"

Lori Lee felt as if Rick had slapped her in the face. His scorn shouldn't have hurt her, but it did. He had deliberately meant to be cruel.

"I hardly think you can compare my relationship with Powell to your relationship with Angie," Lori Lee told him.

"You don't think so? Well, I do. Powell Goodman gives you what you want, doesn't he? You date him because he fulfills your requirements for a boyfriend. Same thing goes for me. Angie gives me what I want, fulfilling my requirements for a girlfriend."

Lori Lee stared at him, her teeth clenched, her hands shaking, as she willed herself not to cry in front of Rick.

He could tell she was on the verge of falling apart. Whether she was about to cry or go into a raging fit, he wasn't sure. But either way, he knew he had gotten to her. Upset her. Maybe even hurt her.

Good. If he had to hurt like this, then she should be hurting, too. If he couldn't find any peace, then he wasn't going to let her find any, either.

Breaking their stare-off, Rick turned and walked to the front door, then paused briefly. With his hand on the doorknob, he looked over his shoulder. "You couldn't tell me you don't want me, could you, honey?" He left the door ajar when he exited the studio.

Lori Lee stormed across the room, slammed the door and let out a wounded growl. How could she ever have had a kind, compassionate thought when it came to Rick Warrick? The man was beneath contempt. He was every bit as vile and vulgar and uncivilized now as he'd been at eighteen.

And heaven help her, she still wanted him, more now than ever before.

Downing the last swig of coffee, Rick screwed the lid back on the empty thermos, then set it on the table. He looked at the ten-dollar plastic wristwatch he always wore at work. Eleven o'clock. He'd told Powell Goodman that he could come over tonight and take a look at his restored 'Vette. Goodman had said he'd bring by a check for payment in full, and if he was completely pleased with the job Rick had done, he would recommend him to his friends and acquaintances.

Rick had every confidence in his abilities. If there was one thing he knew as well as he knew the heating and air-conditioning business, it was cars. Especially old cars. Classics. Someday, if he ever had the money, he'd like to own a few himself. Maybe a 'Vette, like Goodman's, as well as a '65 Mustang and a '56 Chevy.

While waiting for Goodman, he might as well cleanup. He'd already cleared away his tools and put them in his truck. Rick removed his coveralls and placed them in his gym bag, then rolled up the sleeves of his faded green corduroy work shirt.

A car drove up outside. Must be Goodman, Rick thought. He turned on the faucets, picked up a jar of GoJo, covered his hands and forearms and began scrubbing. A car door slammed, then a second door. Goodman wasn't alone. Maybe he'd brought along a buddy, someone who was interested in hiring Rick to restore one of his classic vehicles.

The metal door to the garage opened. The cool March night air drifted in before the door closed.

"Be with you in a minute, Goodman," Rick said. "I was just cleaning up."

"Take your time," Powell told him. "We'll just take a look at my little beauty here. If she runs as good as she looks, I'll be very pleased."

"Believe me, your 'Vette is in top condition. The motor purrs like a satisfied woman." Rick unwound several paper towels from the roll lying by the sink, then turned around as he dried his hands.

He felt as if he'd been poleaxed in the stomach. There, beside an immaculately attired Powell Goodman, stood Lori Lee Guy, breathtaking in her gold velvet skirt and matching jacket.

"Sorry about that comparison," Rick said. "I didn't know you had a lady with you." Rick surveyed Lori Lee from head to toe, his gaze lingering over the full, round swell of her breasts.

"Hey, you two know each other, don't you?" Powell questioned his date. "Didn't you say he's got a kid in one of your classes?"

"Yes, Rick and I know each other." Lori Lee tilted her chin regally as she looked directly at Rick. "His daughter, Darcie, is one of my star pupils."

Powell caressed the 'Vette's front fender. "My old man bought this car new and he let me borrow it on special occasions when I was a kid. Remember when I picked you up in it for the senior prom? I was the envy of every guy in the county. There I was, eighteen, driving a '59 'Vette and escorting Miss DHS."

"That was years ago," Lori Lee said. "Fourteen years, to be exact."

Rick hadn't been around fourteen years ago. He hadn't seen Lori Lee crowned Miss DHS, but he'd heard about it. Eve wrote him on a regular basis while he was in the army, often filling him in on all the local hometown news. She'd even sent him a clipping of Lori Lee's wedding picture that had appeared in the *Times Daily*. He had memorized how she looked in her satin dress and sheer veil before he ripped the clipping into tiny pieces. Later he'd gone out, gotten drunk and slept with some blond chick whose name he couldn't remember.

"I'd like to take this baby for a test run tonight, but Lori Lee's not in the mood." Powell slipped his arm around her waist and pulled her against his side. "Are you, darling?"

Watching Rick look at Powell's arm around her waist made Lori Lee want to pull away from her date, but she didn't. She was not going to allow Rick to intimidate her. He had no claim on her. She was a free woman, and he had no right to look at her as if she had betrayed him.

Powell pulled out his wallet, removed a folded check and

held it out to Rick. "I'll take your word for it that she runs as good as she looks. After all, you wouldn't try to do a number on me, would you, Warrick? I'm the man whose money—" he waved the check around in the air "—is going to help you buy old Bobo Lewis's business."

Squirming out of Powell's grasp, Lori Lee sauntered up and down alongside the 'Vette, running a smoothing hand over the satiny new paint job. "Actually, Powell, the money you owe Rick is his, not yours. From the looks of this car, I'd say he earned every penny."

"Well, aren't you a little democrat tonight, taking up for the working man." Powell handed Rick the check. "You should be flattered that Lori Lee jumped to your defense. But then she's always championed the underdog." Powell gazed at her with adoration in his big, blue eyes. "That's one of the reasons I love her so."

Rick took the check, mumbled a unconvincing thanks and tossed the keys to Powell. "Start her up if you'd like."

"I know I promised we'd be here only a minute," Powell told Lori Lee. "But I've just got to do this." He jumped in the car. "Lori Lee didn't even want to stop by here with me. I had to practically twist her arm, and then when we got here, she wanted to stay outside in the car."

"Maybe the lady didn't want to get her pretty outfit dirty," Rick said. "She doesn't seem the type who likes to go slumming."

Powell laughed, the loud guffaws sounding unusually loud in the large, airy garage. "Well, darling, even a grease monkey like Warrick knows a real lady when he sees one."

Lori Lee looked at Rick, trying to telepathically convey to him that she didn't think and feel about him the way Powell did. She might belong to the same social set, but she really wasn't a snob.

But Rick's cold, cynical stare told her that he had no sympathy for her awkward position, that he saw her for the phony she was.

While Powell played with his expensive toy, Lori Lee

could not help comparing her date with his mechanic. Powell Goodman was a handsome man, with sandy brown hair and mustache, and huge, flirty blue eyes. Tonight he wore one of his many tailored suits that fit his tall, slender body to perfection. There was an air of elegance, good breeding and old money that surrounded Powell. He was quite a catch, and she'd been told by more than one woman just how lucky she was to be dating him.

A. K. Warrick was handsome, too, but in a darker, harder, more powerful way. He was rugged, raw and earthy, his very essence reeking of masculine strength and sensual danger. She'd never seen him wearing anything except faded jeans that hugged his tight butt.

Where Powell's hair was short and neatly styled, Rick's curled about his collar in unruly strands. Where Powell was clean shaven except for his perfectly trimmed mustache, Rick's lean face always showed signs of a five-o'clock shadow.

The two men were an amazing contrast in opposites. Powell was the man everyone expected her to eventually marry. Even Powell thought that sooner or later he'd wear down her resistance. But as well suited as their friends thought they were, they really weren't. Lori Lee didn't love Powell. And she didn't want him. Not the way she wanted Rick.

She hadn't realized how intensely she and Rick were staring at each other until Powell got out of the 'Vette, draped his arm over her shoulders and said, "What's going on here? Did I miss something? Did Warrick say something to upset you, darling? You two are staring daggers at each other."

Lori Lee laughed, the sound shrill and unnatural. "Don't be silly. You're imagining things. Rick's been a perfect gentleman."

"He'd better be when he's around my girl, if he knows what's good for him."

The pulse in Rick's throat throbbed. He uncurled his

balled fists and shoved them into his front pockets. Lori Lee knew he was on the verge of exploding. If the situation hadn't been so deadly serious, she would have laughed at the thought of Powell taking on Rick. Was the man insane? Rick Warrick could beat the hell out of Powell, with one hand tied behind his back.

"Powell, we'd better be going," Lori Lee said. "You did promise we'd stay only a minute."

"She's bossy," Powell said, hugging her close. "But I love her, anyway."

Lori Lee guided Powell to the exit, then paused, turned her head and glanced back at Rick. "Powell, you forgot to tell Rick about Terry Wilbanks's GTO."

"Oh, yeah. At the party we attended tonight, Terry was telling us about an old GTO he recently bought. When he said he was looking for somebody to restore it for him, Lori Lee told him about your working on my 'Vette."

"Terry said he'd give you a call sometime next week." Lori Lee smiled at Rick, but when she saw the cold, heartless expression on his face, her smile faded quickly.

"It seems I owe you my thanks," Rick said mockingly. "It was nice of you to send some work my way."

Lori Lee turned her head sharply, no longer able to bear seeing the anger and ridicule in Rick's eyes. If not for Powell's steadying arm around her, she would have fallen when she tripped in her haste to escape.

After Powell drove her home, Lori Lee gave him a half-hearted good-night kiss at the door, pleading a headache as an excuse not to invite him in. Always the gentleman, he acquiesced to her wishes. Once inside the safety of the foyer, she slumped down on the bottom step of the staircase and cried until her eyes were red and swollen.

The grandfather clock in the hallway struck one in the morning. Lori Lee had taken a warm bath, fixed herself a cup of herbal tea and listened to her CD of soothing chants. But nothing worked. She was wide-awake and miserable.

Even Tyke was restless. He kept watching her, a sad, sympathetic look in his big brown eyes.

She had done everything she could to keep Powell from taking her by the garage to see his car. Everything except tell him the real reason she didn't want to go with him. What would Powell have thought if she'd told him that she couldn't be in the same room with Rick Warrick without wanting to throw herself into his arms and beg him to make love to her? Powell would have been shocked senseless, that's what. Lori Lee chuckled softly. She'd never acted like a wanton hussy with Powell or any other man. Only with Rick.

Rick. The last man on earth she should want. What did they have in common except their raging desire for each other?

Only Darcie. Rick's daughter. The child Lori Lee wished was hers.

The doorbell rang again and again, as if someone's finger was stuck to the buzzer. Tyke cocked his head, raised his ears straight up and barked. No one paid a social call at such an ungodly hour, Lori Lee thought. This had to mean bad news.

Adjusting the belt around her silk robe, she hurried to the door, with Tyke traipsing behind her. Taking the proper safety precaution, she peered through the viewfinder.

"Oh, my God," she murmured.

Rick Warrick stood on her front porch, his index finger repeatedly jabbing the doorbell button. He shouldn't have come here, especially not at this time of night. What on earth would her neighbors think if they saw him or if they noticed his beat-up old truck parked in her driveway?

"Go away, Rick. I don't want to see you. Not tonight."

"Open the damn door, Lori Lee. I'm not leaving."

Knowing how relentless Rick could be, she realized that sooner or later she'd either have to allow him to come in or she'd have to call the police.

She unlocked the door, eased it open and confronted her after-midnight gentleman caller. "What do you want?"

Hovering in the doorway, he visually explored her body, his gaze caressing her silk-covered curves. "Do you really want me to answer that question?"

When her face paled, Rick laughed. "Thought not. Actually, I drove by to see if Goodman was still here. I figured he might be spending the night. I'm a glutton for punishment, honey. I didn't get enough pain from seeing him touch you, from listening to him claim you as his girl or from watching him play the lord of the manor to my lowly peasant."

"Please, Rick, don't do this. Not to yourself and not to me." It took every ounce of her willpower to keep from putting her arms around him and comforting the ache she heard in his voice, from trying to erase the agony she saw in his dark eyes.

Stepping inside, he pushed her backward, then slammed the door behind him. Sniffing Rick's boots, Tyke checked out the man who had invaded his home in the middle of the night.

"We can't go on this way, Lori Lee," Rick said. "It's killing me."

She knew exactly how he felt. Wanting him the way she did and not being with him was killing her, too. She couldn't deny her desire for him; the need was too strong.

"We're no good for each other," she told him. "If we give in to what we want, we could destroy ourselves. I have to think of myself and what's best for me. You're the wrong answer to my problems. And you have to think of yourself, of what you're working so hard to achieve. And of Darcie's future."

"I can't think about anything except how much I want you. Day and night. Awake or asleep. Having you so close and not being able to take you in my arms is driving me crazy." He moved forward. She retreated. "You can run, honey, but you can't escape me. I'm in your blood, as surely as you're in mine."

"And what about Angie Clemmons? Is she in your blood, too?" Lori Lee glared at him, hating him for being able to find solace in another woman's bed.

"You have no reason to be jealous of Angie. She doesn't mean a thing to me."

"You have sex with a lot of women who mean nothing to you, don't you, Rick? I don't want to be just another one of those women."

He grabbed her by the back of her neck. She stood there paralyzed by his heated glare. Sensing his mistress's stress, Tyke growled a warning.

"I haven't had sex with another woman since the night I made love to you in the garage," Rick told her. "You're what I want, what I've always wanted."

"Why should I believe you?"

"Have you had sex with anyone since that night?" he asked, lowering his head until his lips lightly brushed hers.

"That's none of your business," she said. Still holding her by the nape of her neck, he ran his other hand down her shoulder and over her breast, lingering at her stomach. He spread out his fingers over her belly, the tips almost touching her mound. "No," she admitted. "I haven't had sex with anyone else."

"I could have had Angie or a dozen more just like her," Rick said. "Just like you could have taken Goodman or any other man you wanted to your bed. But sex with anyone else would have been useless. It would have been like giving a man dying of thirst saltwater to drink."

"Rick, this is a mistake." She pushed against his chest, but the effort was weak and halfhearted.

Tyke growled again, a bit more ferocious. Lori Lee spoke to him in a soft voice, reassuring him that she was safe. But she knew she wasn't safe. She was in danger of losing her heart.

Rick drew her up against his body, pressing her intimately against his arousal. "There's no use fighting it, honey. Nobody can give you what you need but me."

Sucking in her breath, she melted into him, then lifted herself on tiptoe, offering him her mouth. His tongue circled her lips. She moaned. He nibbled on her lower lip. She whimpered.

"Say the words, baby," he commanded, his hand tightening on her neck. "Tell me you want me."

"I want you, Rick. I want you." She kissed his mouth. "I want you." She kissed his chin. "I want you." She licked a moist trail down his throat. "I want all of you."

Seven

"This time, it's going to be the way I've always wanted it to be. No quick tumble. I plan to stay all night and take you every way a man can take a woman. By morning, you'll be so completely mine, you'll never let another man touch you." Reaching between their bodies, he untied her belt and opened her robe, revealing the front of her naked body. He sucked in a raspy breath. "God, you're one beautiful woman!"

A dragging sensation encompassed her body, pulling her into a silken web of promise. "Rick?"

"What do you want, Lori Lee? Do you want me to touch you?" His big hand hovered over her breast.

"Yes, please, Rick. Touch me." If he wanted to hear her beg, then she would beg. She needed his hands and mouth on her body. She would do whatever he asked of her.

He eased the robe off her shoulders, completely exposing her full breasts. Her rosy nipples peaked when he looked at them. He rubbed his index finger over the tip of one. She cried out as an all-consuming, hungry ache tightened her breasts. He rubbed her other nipple.

As an involuntary tremor shimmied through her, she gasped several times, then released a sighing breath. She could smell Rick. Musty, masculine power blended with the fresh, clean scent of the soap he'd used when he showered.

He smiled, loving the way she reacted to his touch. Cupping the heaviness of her breasts in his hands, he tormented their crests with the rotating movement of his thumbs. Closing her eyes as she tossed her head back, Lori Lee leaned against the wall behind her, flattening her palms against the smooth surface.

With the sleeves of her red silk robe hanging about her elbows, the hem dragging the floor, she opened her eyes slowly, staring up at Rick with a sleepy, sexy, needy look. "I want to touch you, too."

His gaze traveled the length of her body, halting momentarily to examine the nest of blond curls at the apex between her thighs. Then he lifted his gaze to meet hers. Reaching out, he prized her hands away from the wall and laid them on his chest.

With nervous fingers rushing at the task, she unbuttoned his gray cotton shirt and jerked it free from his jeans. She spread her hands over his naked chest, curling her fingers in his thick, black chest hair.

Wondrous, delicious feelings spiraled through her. Touching Rick was such a pleasure. He was hard, muscled man, his flesh warm and tempting. She inched her fingertips up his chest and onto his broad shoulders.

Was there anything more purely, primordially male than the breadth of a man's shoulders? The look and feel of something so powerfully masculine enticed all that was feminine within Lori Lee to respond. Her heartbeat accelerated. Her breasts felt tight and very heavy. And the core of her body tingled with hot, moist anticipation.

Growling deep in his throat, Rick speared his fingers through her hair and captured the back of her head. Lori Lee gasped at the primitive, possessive gesture, but didn't protest his right to claim her. Giving herself over to him, trusting him not to hurt her, she gazed up at him, allowing him to see the yearning in her eyes.

This was what she'd wanted since she was seventeen and Rick kissed her for the first time. This exquisite, tormenting desire was what she'd been born to feel—but with only one man.

He trembled, his need for Lori Lee so strong it frightened him. Holding her head, he leaned down and brought her face upward to meet his. Her hot, womanly scent, combined with her expensive perfume, intoxicated him. Clamping his mouth down over hers, he kissed her ravenously. He had spent a lifetime wanting and needing this. Wanting and needing Lori Lee in a way no amount of sex with other women had ever been able to satisfy. It was as if she had been created for him and him alone. Only his touch could awaken the sleeping beauty of passion within her; and only she could bring him the ecstasy he had sought and never found.

While he thrust his tongue into her mouth with a driving rhythm, he pressed her against the wall, trapping her there with his big, hard body. Sliding his hand between her legs, he palmed her, then squeezed her mound. She shivered uncontrollably. Prizing her thighs apart, he stroked her intimately with his thumb as he inserted his fingers into her hot, clutching body. A storm of raging hunger ravaged her senses. Grasping his shoulders, she moaned into his mouth.

Rick pulled her hands off his shoulders and eased her robe down and off, letting it pool about her feet in a red silk cloud. He kissed her chin, her neck and both distended nipples. His sex grew harder and heavier with every little moan and cry she uttered.

"I've dreamed of touching you this way," he told her. Bending his knees and lowering his head, he licked damp circles over her stomach. "I've thought about tasting you. Every inch of you. Eating my fill of your sweetness."

He delved his tongue into her navel, then withdrew, only to repeat the process several times. Lori Lee's knees weakened. She swayed unsteadily on her feet.

Rick reached up, grabbed her hands and placed them on his shoulders, showing her how to brace herself for the upcoming assault. Burying his face in her soft, musky curls, he pleasured her with his mouth. When she clawed at his shoulders, pleading with him to end the torture, he increased the pressure and speed of his strokes until he felt her body tighten and release. She screamed as fulfillment erupted inside her, shaking her so badly that she slumped over, her bones becoming liquid.

She was still gasping for air and trembling with tiny aftershocks of release when Rick lifted her in his arms and carried her up the stairs. Resting her head on his shoulder, she clung to him. She had never known anything so shamefully, sinfully erotic as the sweet, intimate loving Rick had given her.

"Which room is yours?" he asked.

Still surrounded by a fog of hazy satiation, Lori Lee couldn't speak. She pointed to her open bedroom door. Rick carried her into the golden room, lighted by two bedside sconces that cast the elegantly feminine room into soft, subdued shadows. Leaning over, he lifted her up and into the middle of the undraped four-poster brass bed, laying her on top of the handmade crocheted coverlet. With his knees pressed against the edge of the bed and his hands braced on either side of her, Rick worshiped her with his gaze. Adoring her with his hungry eyes, he nuzzled her neck and whispered softly, "I'll make you forget any other man who's ever made love to you in this bed."

"There hasn't been anyone else." She caressed the hard, chiseled line of his jaw, loving the feel of his heavy, day's growth of beard. "Not in this bed, this room or this house."

"Not even Goodman?" The thought of her with that man ripped at his guts.

"No one," she vowed.

He lifted himself up and off her, quickly divested himself of his clothes and came back to her, covering her body with his. Nestling his throbbing arousal between her legs, he took her in his arms and kissed her over and over again, murmuring boldly erotic words to her, telling her with basic, earthy phrases how he felt and what he wanted. She welcomed his raw, untamed passion, at first submitting to and then becoming a full participant in the glorious orgy of kissing.

She swept his big body with her hands, settling her fingertips on his tiny bronze nipples, teasing them unmercifully. Reaching beneath her, he lifted her buttocks and brought her upward to meet the demanding steel of his arousal. The inner walls of her femininity clutched and released, preparing for his entrance.

"Please, Rick. Don't wait. Take me now." She longed to feel him buried inside her, thrusting to the hilt, filling her completely. She wanted—no, she needed—his masterful possession.

He pressed himself against her. She moaned. "You want me?" He taunted her with the mocking thrusts of his body, promising but withholding. "You want this?"

Arching up to meet him, her body undulating pleadingly, Lori Lee grasped his firm, tight buttocks. "Yes, I want you."

"All of me?" He rose over her, separating their bodies as he looked down at her and smiled devilishly.

"Yes, Rick, yes!"

"Then take me, honey. Take all of me."

He entered her hard and fast, his body throbbing painfully with need. She gasped at the sensation of having him so deeply, fully embedded within her. His possession was all she had wanted and more. They made love. Hot. Wild. Furious. Turning and twisting. Thrusting and retreating.

The bed trembled with the force of their savage mating. Their fervent, vulgar words of passion fueled the fires burning so turbulently within them.

Lori Lee screamed with release as spasm after spasm of pleasure shook her and the dark, sweet oblivion of completion surrounded her. When her wet heat tightened around him, urging his body to follow hers, he thrust one final time. Groaning, shaking, sweat dripping from his big body, Rick exploded as a hard, shattering release claimed him. He lay atop her, hot, sticky and heavy. But she loved the feel of him still inside her, and draped her arms around his waist, holding him tenderly.

"I'm too heavy," he told her, then eased to her side, pulling her damp, shivering body close to him.

Curling up against him, she kissed his shoulder. "What just happened was... I don't know how to describe how I feel. Nothing like this has ever... Oh, Rick, Rick."

He kissed her, his lips soft and giving on hers. "You told me how you felt, honey, without saying a word. Your body said it all for you."

"You're so wonderful." She rose on one elbow and gazed down at him. Big, hard and beautiful beyond words. A body thickly muscled. Long arms and legs sprinkled with curly black hair, a thick patch encircling his impressive manhood.

"You're the one who's wonderful." He kissed her on the nose, then rolled them over to the edge of the bed.

She giggled and squirmed when he lifted her in his arms and stood, carrying her through the open bathroom door.

"What are you doing?" she asked, clinging to him.

He eased her down the length of his body, then held her by her waist while he turned on the shower. "We're both sweaty and smell of sex," he told her. "We're going to take a shower, then go back to bed and start all over again."

True to his world, Rick lathered her with scented soap and washed her thoroughly, acquainting himself with every inch of her body. And when he completed his task, she returned the favor, finding great enjoyment in scrubbing him from head to toe. She lingered on the part of his body that fascinated her the most, giving it special attention. By the time they had dried each other, Rick's hardness beckoned to her, tempting her beyond reason.

She led him back to her bed, and this time she took charge, teasing and tormenting him with her hands and tongue. She licked and sucked, coaxing his body, taking him to the very edge before retreating. When he couldn't bear another minute of her torture, he lifted her up and over his body, and thrust upward into her welcoming heat.

Crying out with pleasure when he filled her, she straddled his hips and positioned herself like an equestrian preparing for the main event. He bucked up, plunging higher, asking her to take him completely. She accepted him, settling around him and leaning over just enough to offer him her breasts. And while she rode him hard and fast, pushing herself closer and closer to completion, he suckled her breasts and stroked her hips. Then, within seconds of each other, Lori Lee and Rick experienced the longest, hottest, most earth-shattering moments they'd ever known.

Keeping his earlier promise to take her every way a man can take a woman, Rick explored countless avenues of erotic pleasure, taking Lori Lee to places she'd never known existed—to heights he had never achieved with any other woman. For both of them, these were precious stolen hours of bliss. No past. No future. Only the wondrous, glorious present.

When dawn's first light appeared in the eastern sky, Rick and Lori Lee cried out their pleasure one more time, then lay in each other's arms, replete and totally spent. Tyke rested snugly on a small floral rug beside the bed.

"I should go," Rick whispered against her breast.

"No." She held him to her warm body.

"My old truck is parked in your driveway," he told her. "People will know I'm here, and you don't want that."

"What if I told you I don't care if the whole town knows you spent the night here with me?" She caressed the long, silky strands of his hair.

"I'd say you're lying to yourself, honey." He kissed one rosy nipple and smiled when he saw it pucker into a tight bud. "Besides, you're still caught up in the aftereffects of a lot of great sex."

Lori Lee yanked his hair, pulling his head up so that he faced her. "Are you saying this was a one-night affair? Or are you suggesting we sneak around and keep our relationship a secret?"

Pulling out of her grasp, Rick sat up in bed and grabbed her chin. "You know as well as I do that we can't control this thing between us, so I suppose how we handle it is up to you. If you want to be lovers in private and little more than strangers in public, then I'll swallow my pride and deal with it somehow."

"I'm not quite ready to announce to the whole world that we're lovers," she admitted. "But I'm not ashamed of you—of us—if that's what you're thinking. It's just that we started our relationship off backward. We've become lovers before dating and becoming friends."

"Are you saying you want us to date?" he asked.

"I know you don't have a lot of spare time, but you and I and Darcie could do things together. That way you and I could get to know each other better, and you could still spend time with Darcie."

"Just what do you have in mind?" He kissed her on the tip of her nose. "Taking my daughter to Disney movies and you and me making out in the dark theater?"

"I'm serious." She jabbed him in the ribs. "I want you and Darcie to come to dinner on Sunday." When she looked at him and saw him grinning at her, she slapped him playfully. "This all happened too fast, and I'm not sure of myself or my feelings. I want to back up a little and take things a little slower.''

"Yeah, I know what you mean. As much as I wanted you, as many times I dreamed of becoming your lover, all this doesn't seem quite real." Cupping her face in his hands, he stared at her. "Don't you think I know that I'm not good enough for you, that you could have your pick of men."

She covered his lips with her fingertips. "Hush. Don't talk crazy. I'm not the perfect woman you think I am. There are things about me—"

He kissed her, thoroughly yet tenderly. When he ended the kiss they were both breathless.

"Darcie and I will be here for Sunday dinner. You just tell me what time."

"One o'clock." She caressed his cheek, then let her fingers trail down his neck and onto his chest. "We're going to date and get to know each other and see if there's more to what we feel than sexual attraction. Agreed?"

"There's something about this deal I'm not going to like, isn't there?" he asked, shaking his head. "We're not going to have sex for a while. That's the catch, isn't it?"

"As long as we're having sex, how will we ever know if there's more to our relationship?"

"Damn!"

"It will be just as difficult for me as it will be for you," she said. "All the while you'll be wanting me, I'll be wanting you just as much."

He grunted. "Believe me, honey, doing without is going to hurt a lot more than you think it is." He flung the cover away from her naked body, reached out and flicked his nail across her nipple. Lori Lee cried out as pure sensual sensation shot through her. "See what I mean?"

"Uh-huh." She shoved him down on his back, covered his body with hers and claimed his mouth in a tongue-thrusting kiss.

When she allowed him to come up for air, she said,

"We'll date for six weeks, without having sex, and then we'll decide where to go from there? Agreed?"

"Agreed. But I'm not happy about it." He stroked her naked hip. "Are you too sore to take me again, honey? If you are, I'll understand. But six weeks is a damn long time."

"I'm pretty sore," she admitted. "My body's not used to marathon lovemaking sessions. But since I'll have six weeks to recuperate—"

Rick needed no further inducement. He surged up and into her, wanting to brand her his forever.

By lunchtime, everyone who cared to listen to the latest gossip knew that Rick Warrick's GMC pickup had been parked in Lori Lee Guy's driveway from sometime after midnight until nearly seven o'clock that morning.

A steady stream of browsers entered the Sparkle and Shine shop, chatted with Aunt Birdie and inspected Lori Lee as if looking for some change in her appearance, then exited the building as they whispered to one another.

By the time the twentieth customer came and went without purchasing anything, Aunt Birdie flipped over the Closed sign and locked the front door. She planted her hands on her wide hips, pursed her lips and glared at her niece.

"I demand to know what's going on! People who've never been in this store have dropped by today, and they've all been twittering around like idiots and looking you over from head to toe. It seems that everyone in town knows something I don't know, and I won't have it. Do you hear me? I won't have it!"

"I suppose some of my neighbors saw a pickup truck parked in my driveway from around one last night until seven o'clock this morning." Lori Lee looked her aunt square in the eye without flinching.

"An old, battered, blue GMC pickup truck?" Birdie asked, a hint of a smile on her lips.

"Yes."

Birdie scurried behind the checkout counter and grasped Lori Lee's hands. "You know that confession is good for the soul, don't you, sugar?"

Nodding agreement, Lori Lee smiled. "I'm having an affair with Rick Warrick."

Birdie squeezed Lori Lee's hands tightly. "Well, glory be. It's about time."

"Aunt Birdie!"

"I know it'll take your friends time to come around, to accept Rick, but once they realize what a fine man he is, they'll change their minds about him. And you and I have enough money and clout in this community to help things along. I could give Rick the money to buy Bobo's business as a wedding present for the two of you." Birdie patted her hands together like a gleeful child.

"Calm down, Aunt Birdie. You misunderstood—"

Disregarding her niece's attempt to explain the situation, Birdie rattled on and on. "This is all so wonderful. I've known all along, of course, that the two of you were meant for each other. And now, you'll have that precious little Darcie for your very own. You will make the most beautiful bride, and Darcie can be your flower girl, and...oh, dear me, it's already the middle of March. You are planning a June wedding, aren't you? I don't think I can pull together anything really spectacular before then."

Lori Lee grabbed her aunt's fluttering hands. "Rick and I aren't getting married. We're having an affair. Sort of. We're going to date and see if there's more to our relationship than great sex."

"What more do you need?" Birdie raised her eyebrows inquisitively.

"I need to be in love before I marry a man," Lori Lee said. "And I have to know that a man loves me enough to accept the fact that I can never have children."

"Are you trying to tell me that you and Rick aren't in love? Well, don't bother. You'll never convince me. You were in love with him when you were seventeen and he was mad about you."

"Sexual attraction isn't love," Lori Lee said.

"Yes, well, maybe it isn't, but sexual attraction is a good seventy-five percent of it, my girl. I should know. I've been in love half a dozen times in my life and I married five of those lovers."

"Rick and I have agreed to date for the next six weeks and really get to know each other."

"Without having sex?"

"Yes, without having sex."

"My Lord! That gorgeous hunk of a man at your disposal and you're going to let him go to waste while you're *dating?* I swear if there wasn't such a strong family resemblance, I'd think they switched babies at the hospital and you aren't really any blood kin to me."

"Rick and I are trying to do the right thing, for both of us. And for Darcie. Rick and I have very little in common. Once we get to know each other, we could be totally incompatible."

"That's the trouble with young people today. They do too much thinking and talking about things none of us are meant to understand. Love is one of those things. You don't fall in love because it's the right thing to do. It just happens. Like getting struck by lightning. And take my word for it, truly great sex is a rare gift to be treasured. It can be the strongest bond between a man and a woman."

"You may be right, Aunt Birdie. But I'm not going to risk ruining three lives without being absolutely sure Rick and I can build a future together."

At precisely one o'clock on Sunday afternoon, Rick and Darcie appeared at Lori Lee's front door. Darcie wore her church clothes, a cute little black-and-white checkered dress, accented with a red leather belt. Rick, who confessed he didn't own a suit, wore a pair of khaki slacks, a blue button-down shirt, without a tie, and a navy blue sport coat.

He still looked as if he needed a shave and a haircut, but those deficiencies in his appearance only added to his aura of masculine beauty.

Lori Lee's dark purple crepe coatdress clung softly to her curves when she opened the front door and invited her guests into her home.

"Please, come in. Dinner is almost ready. I'm so glad y'all could come."

Tyke came bounding into the foyer, sniffing their Sunday afternoon company. Lori Lee cautioned him to behave himself, but when Darcie knelt to pet him, Tyke licked her in the face.

Darcie giggled. "He gave me a kiss." When she hugged him, he licked her again. "I think he likes me."

"I think he does," Lori Lee said. "Come on into the living room. Tyke will follow us. Believe me, he thinks he's the boss around here."

Darcie looked up adoringly at Lori Lee. "Daddy says that we're going to be dating you, and that means we're going to be spending a lot of time together."

Smiling at Darcie, Lori Lee took the child's hand. "That's right, sweetheart, if it's all right with you."

"Oh, it's fine with me," Darcie said. "You're exactly who I picked out for me and Daddy. The first time I saw you, I knew you were the one for us."

"Now, Darcie, I told you that Lori Lee and I are just dating. That's all," Rick reminded his daughter.

"Yeah, I know. But people always have to go out on a few dates before they get married, don't they?"

Lori Lee glared at Rick, her blue eyes questioning him. He shrugged his shoulders as if saying, What am I supposed to do with her?

"Well, Darcie, would you and your father like to look around a bit or watch some television or listen to some CDs while I put dinner on the table?" Lori Lee asked.

"I'd like to help you," Darcie said. "Trey and Mark help Aunt Eve. They set the table and she lets them put stuff in the dishwasher after they eat. She lets me help, too, when I stay with them."

"Darcie, Lori Lee isn't used to having a little girl handle her china and crystal and—"

"I'd love to have your help," Lori Lee said, then glanced at Rick. "And for your information, Mr. Warrick, we aren't having our meal in the dining room and I'm not using china and crystal. I thought it would be more cozy in the kitchen, just the three of us."

"In that case, maybe Darcie and I both can help," Rick said.

After washing their hands, the three of them set the table with Lori Lee's sunny yellow everyday earthenware, simple shiny stainless flatware and glasses decorated with a tiny yellow and white daisy design. Sitting in the center of the oak table, a small bouquet of yellow roses and white daisies caught Darcie's eye and she asked if yellow roses were Lori Lee's favorite flower. She said yes, and saw the sad look in Rick's eyes.

Someday, maybe, Lori Lee thought, she would show Rick the single yellow rose she had pressed in her favorite book of poetry. The rose he'd thought she wouldn't want.

Darcie asked to say grace before they ate. Then, during the meal of crisp, tender pork chops, fried potatoes, corn on the cob and lima beans, she was very careful to remember her manners, except when it came to talking with her mouth full of food. Darcie's exuberant chatter amazed Rick. Usually she was shy around other people, a magpie only around him.

Tyke wandered around the table, looking up at the humans pleadingly, as if to say, I'm starving, although his plump little body denied the accusation. Lori Lee dropped a bite of meat into the dog's open mouth.

"I've spoiled him shamelessly," she admitted. "Deanie says I love him too much and that he has me trained instead of the other way around."

"Maybe she's right," Rick said. "But I think a little

pampering is a good thing. I figure its better to be loved too much than not enough.''

Lori Lee sensed that he was talking about himself, and the long, lonely years of neglect he'd endured as a young boy.

"You love me too much, don't you, Daddy? 'Cause I'm your bestest girl.'' Darcie's smile beamed brightly as she gazed worshipfully at her father.

"You bet, sweetie,'' he said.

The look of love in Rick's eyes when he spoke to his daughter was almost more than Lori Lee could bear to see. She envied both father and child. If Darcie was hers, she would love her *too much*, just the way Rick did. And despite her uncertainty concerning her feelings for Rick, she couldn't help wondering how it would feel to have such a passionate man truly love her *too much*.

After lunch, Lori Lee tied a bright yellow apron around Darcie, the hem hitting her ankles, then put on a matching apron.

Once again Rick marveled at the unbelievable resemblance between Lori Lee and Darcie. Even he, if he didn't know better, would think them mother and daughter. A hot, searing pain ripped through him at the thought of how much he wished Darcie was Lori Lee's child.

The three of them cleared the table, loaded the dishwasher and scrubbed the pots and pans. Then after cleanup duty, Lori Lee brought out some games she kept at the studio for days when the students had parties. She allowed Darcie to choose her favorite, which was Clue. Rick thought the game might be a little too advanced for his daughter, but she proved him wrong when she won two of the four games they played.

Since it was a sunny day, Lori Lee suggested a romp in the backyard for Tyke while Darcie performed her recently perfected baton routine for her father.

Rick and Lori Lee sat on the back steps, Lori Lee's tape player providing the musical accompaniment for Darcie's high-stepping dance number. The child gloried in the attention she received. Tears of happiness gathered in her eyes when the two adults applauded enthusiastically, Rick cheering and Lori Lee repeating the word *perfect* over and over again.

Later in the day, they popped popcorn and watched a video. Darcie's favorite, *Beauty and the Beast.*

"May I lie on the floor?" Darcie asked. "I like to watch TV propped up on pillows."

Before Rick could protest, Lori Lee tossed three pillows off the sofa onto the floor. After building a nest for her and Tyke, Darcie waited eagerly for the movie to begin. Lori Lee prepared the VCR, then sat on the crimson-and-cream pinstriped sofa. Still standing, Rick nodded at the sofa, asking permission to join her. She patted the cushion beside her, issuing Rick an invitation.

Sitting, he draped his arm over the sofa back, directly behind Lori Lee. All the while his daughter watched the movie, he watched the woman at his side. From time to time, Lori Lee would glance at him and smile, but for the most part, she concentrated on the movie and on exchanging comments about the story with Darcie.

"You know a lot about kids, don't you?" Rick wondered why a woman who obviously adored children didn't have any of her own. He knew she'd been married for five years, certainly long enough to have started a family.

"I work with children, remember?"

"Yeah, I know, but it's more than that." He could not resist the temptation to touch her. Just a simple, nonsexual touch. A light brush of his fingertips over her cheek. "You'd make a wonderful mother."

For a few timeless seconds, Lori Lee couldn't breathe. She felt as if some giant foot was pressing down on her chest. "Thank you," she finally managed to say.

He realized he'd said something wrong, but he couldn't figure out exactly what. Was it possible that she really didn't want a child of her own?

He decided changing the subject was the best course of action. "Tell me a little bit about this recital deal that's coming up in a couple of weeks."

"Aren't you interested in the movie?" she asked.

"Is that your way of telling me to be quiet so you can enjoy *Beauty and the Beast?*"

"It's my favorite fairy tale, too. This tape happens to belong to me. It's my personal copy."

When the movie ended, Lori Lee was snuggled against Rick, his arm draped around her shoulders. Rick hit the rewind button on the remote control, then glanced down at Darcie and Tyke.

"Take a look," he said. "Our little beauty has fallen asleep."

Darcie lay with her head nestled on one of the pillows and her body curled into a ball. Tyke slept contentedly at her side.

"Does she often take late-afternoon naps?" Lori Lee asked.

"No, not usually. But she was so excited about our big date with you that she woke me up at five o'clock this morning."

"Should we let her sleep awhile?"

"Yeah, don't wake her yet. Let her get a little nap," Rick suggested. "You and I could talk—" he caressed Lori Lee's neck "—or kiss—" he brushed her lips with his "—or go in the kitchen and find out just how sturdy that oak table is."

"You're shameless." Lori Lee giggled softly, slapping at Rick's grasping hands. "No sex. Remember our agreement."

He nuzzled her neck. "It's been only a few days and I'm already dying to be inside you again, honey." He whispered the words against her warm flesh.

Lori Lee tried to get up off the sofa, but Rick dragged her down onto his lap. She struggled for a few minutes, then gave in and put her arms around his neck.

"Behave yourself," she warned him.

He undulated his hips gently, just enough so that his obvious arousal rubbed against her buttocks. Gasping, she tried to get up again. "Sit still, baby. I promise I won't let things get out of hand. I know my little girl is right over there." He nodded toward Darcie.

"Rick?"

"What?" God, how he'd longed to hold her in his arms, feel the sweetness of her lush body close to him. But this wasn't going to be enough to satisfy him. He needed to make love to her. Today. Tonight. Tomorrow. And the day after that, and the day after that.

He heard Lori Lee's voice, but he didn't understand what she was saying. All he could do was feel and want and need.

She slapped his shoulder. "Rick! You aren't listening to me."

"Sorry, honey, what did you say?"

"I asked you if Powell Goodman has been to see you."

"He picked up his 'Vette the other morning. I haven't seen him since. Why?"

"The whole town knows about us," she said.

"Yeah, I know. Eve told me that you and I are definitely the talk of Tuscumbia."

"Powell has been saying some pretty stupid things." Lori Lee laid her head on Rick's shoulder. "He's made some threats."

"Yeah, what kind of threats?" Rick asked.

"Just don't get into a fight with him. Okay? He carries a lot of weight in this part of the state, and if he wanted to, he could cause problems for you."

"Let him." Rick squeezed her hip. "If he thinks he's going to scare me away from you, then he'd better think again. I won. He lost. He'd better get use to the idea that you belong to me now."

"I do not belong to you. I don't belong to anyone except myself."

"That's a bunch of feminist garbage and you know it," he told her. "If my daughter wasn't here, I'd show you just how completely you belong to me." When she opened her mouth to protest, he kissed her quickly, then said, "And it works both ways, Lori Lee. I belong to you, too."

"What am I going to do with you, Rick Warrick? You are the most irritating, infuriating man I've ever known."

"You're going to let me really kiss you, and you're going to love it." He lowered his lips to hers. "And while I'm kissing you, you're going to remember what it was like upstairs in that big brass bed of yours, and you're going to ache with wanting me just like I'm already aching."

She accepted the onslaught of his kisses, needing more but willing to take this little slice of paradise he offered. The kiss grew hot and wild. Only the sound of Darcie Warrick's voice brought them to their senses.

"Does this mean what I think it means?" Darcie rubbed her sleepy eyes. Smiling, she gazed up at her father and the woman in his arms.

Tyke roused, lifting his head, sniffing the air.

"Oh, my goodness," Lori Lee moaned as she rested her forehead against Rick's.

Rick eased Lori Lee off his lap and quickly crossed his legs. "What—" he cleared his throat "—what do you think this means?"

"That y'all are in love. On television and in the movies people kiss the way y'all did when they're in love."

"Well, I'll tell you, kiddo," Rick said. "That kiss means that Lori Lee and I like each other an awful lot and we're going to have more dates."

"Aren't y'all in love?" Darcie asked.

"Not exactly," Rick said.

"Why would you kiss Lori Lee like that if you don't love her?"

Rick looked to Lori Lee for help, but she simply smiled and shrugged, as if to say, "You're on your own in answering this one.

Darcie had asked him a damn good question, Rick thought, but one he couldn't truthfully answer. Not for his six-year-old daughter. She wasn't quite old enough for the birds-and-bees discussion. So how did he explain a passionate kiss without mentioning sex?

"Well, Darcie, you see, I...that is, we...Lori Lee and I..." He looked pleadingly at Lori Lee.

She patted her lap, then held open her arms. Darcie rushed across the room, crawled onto Lori Lee's lap and gazed up at her. Following hurriedly, Tyke jumped up on the sofa and rooted his nose against Lori Lee's thigh. She petted him affectionately, murmuring softly to him.

"Grown-ups who like each other enjoy kissing and hugging each other," Lori Lee explained. "I like your father very much and he likes me, but we don't know each other well enough to be in love."

"That's funny," Darcie said. "Because Aunt Eve told me that she and Uncle Tommy fell in love at first sight."

Rick chuckled, then cleared his throat and put a somber look on his face when Lori Lee glared at him.

"Eve and Tommy were very young and they'd never been in love before," Lori Lee said. "But your daddy and I are older and we've both been married to other people, so neither of us wants to rush into anything and make a mistake."

"Are you and Daddy going to hug and kiss each other every time you have a date?"

"Yes, we probably will," Lori Lee admitted.

"Good," Darcie said. "My daddy's a pretty great guy, you know, so I figure if you keep on hugging and kissing him the way you were doing today, then you'll fall in love with him in no time."

An hour later, after Rick and Darcie had left, Lori Lee went over every detail of their first "date." She considered the whole afternoon a success. Rick and his daughter had seemed right at home with her and Tyke, and she had enjoyed their company immensely. Despite being denied the pleasure of having sex with Rick, Lori Lee felt warmly content.

And she'd agreed to a second date with the Warrick family. Rick had invited her to go to McDonald's for supper with them after Darcie's next twirler class.

Eight

"You know I'm on your side." Deanie Webber reclined on the brocade chaise longue in Lori Lee's bedroom. She dangled her brown suede flats on the tips of her toes, then dropped the shoes to the floor. "I'm all for your dating Rick. As a matter of fact, I'm all for your having a raging affair with the man."

Rummaging through her closet, Lori Lee tossed out a pair of rumpled jeans and a faded, plaid flannel shirt. "I know there's a *but* in there somewhere. You didn't stop by at seven o'clock on a Saturday morning just to wish me well."

"You're my best friend," Deanie said. "I don't want to see you get hurt. I remember what a basket case you were right after your divorce from Tory. I know you. You don't do anything by half measures."

Lori Lee removed a pair of dingy tennis shoes from the back of her closet. "Saving these shows it pays to keep old stuff instead of throwing it away."

"Stop trying to change the subject."

"Is that what I'm doing?" Lori Lee asked as she slipped out of her robe. "I thought I was getting ready for a date with Rick."

Deanie watched while Lori Lee put on the ragged jeans and oversize flannel shirt. "What kind of date does a woman have that requires her to dress like a bum and be ready at such an ungodly hour?"

"If it's such an ungodly hour, what are you doing up and over here giving me advice?"

"I'm on my way to an early-bird sale at the mall, so I decided this would be the perfect time to stop by and have a little talk with you."

Lori Lee sat on the edge of her bed, pulled on some heavy cotton socks and eased her feet into a ten-year-old pair of tennis shoes. "If you're here to warn me that Rick Warrick is probably going to break my heart, don't bother. I'm well aware of his reputation with women. We haven't made any commitments to each other. All we're doing is testing the waters, to see if we're suitable for each other."

"Yeah, yeah, yeah. You told me all about this brilliant idea of yours to date Rick for several weeks to see if y'all have anything going for you besides great sex." Deanie bent her knees, crossed her ankles and braced her hands on top of her thighs. "What I don't understand is, if you and Rick share great sex, why do you need anything else if you're just going to have an affair? My guess is that you've got marriage in the back of your mind."

"Lord, you're as bad as Aunt Birdie. She's already planning a June wedding."

"Some people would look the other way if all you want is an affair with Rick, but they wouldn't accept your marrying the man." Deanie rubbed her hands up and down her thighs, then clasped her knees. "There are a few people already on the warpath. Powell Goodman thinks you made him look like a fool, a cuckolded fool and—"

"Powell is not my husband or my fiancé."

"The point I'm trying to make is that you've made Powell an enemy that Rick may have to deal with sooner or later, and Mara Royce is going to give you trouble—big time trouble. She's already stirring a stink with the twirler mothers."

"Name me one twirler mother who likes Mara? Everyone resents her using her husband's and father's wealth and their social position to try to intimidate people." Lori Lee removed a red, button-up knit jacket from a dresser drawer, threw it over her shoulders and loosely tied the sleeves around her neck.

"Mara has spent the past two days contacting every twirler mother to solicit their opinion about your carrying on with a man like Rick Warrick," Deanie said.

"I'm not surprised. My carrying on with Rick wouldn't bother Mara half as much if Rick didn't have a beautiful daughter who has more talent in her little finger than Mara's Steffie has in her whole body." When she headed out into the hall, Lori Lee motioned for Deanie to follow. "Come on downstairs with me. I've got to load up my picnic basket and eat a bite of breakfast before Rick gets here."

Deanie uncrossed her legs, bent over and put on her shoes, then stood and stretched her arms over her head. "You're right about Mara, but that still doesn't mean she's not going to give you hell. And there are some people who'll listen to her, even if they don't like her personally. You know the ones I mean."

"The people she easily intimidates," Lori Lee said, halting in the doorway. "The mothers who are so afraid Mara will exclude their daughters from the list of Steffie's friends."

Rubbing her back as she crossed the room, Deanie walked over and put her arm around her best friend's shoulder. "Look, hon, you know that Phil and I will go to battle for you, and Aunt Birdie is ready to take on the whole world, not only the local powers that be. And I'm sure Eve and Tom Nelson are on our side, but before we gird up our loins and sharpen our swords, I want to make damn sure you know what you're doing.''

Lori Lee raced down the stairs, wanting to escape the hard, cold facts Deanie had presented to her, but she knew she couldn't run away from the truth. She *was* risking a great deal. Her good reputation and several old friendships were on the line, and there was always a possibility that Mara Royce's influence on other parents could hurt her Dixie Twirlers business. And she stood a very real chance of getting her heart broken. No matter how much she wanted things to work out for her and Rick, she knew the odds were against them.

Deanie caught up with Lori Lee in the kitchen, where Lori Lee busied herself packing plastic-and aluminum foil-wrapped items into a large basket.

"If you're going on an early Saturday morning picnic, why are you dressed like Freddie the Freeloader?" Deanie asked.

"I'm not going on a picnic." Lori Lee closed the basket lid, then turned and opened the refrigerator, pulling out a milk jug. "Rick is painting Eve and Tommy's house to earn extra money to pay for Darcie's costumes for the recital and other twirler events during the spring and summer. So I told him if he'd pick me up about seven-thirty, I'd help him paint and we could spend the whole day together." Lori Lee set the milk on the table, then retrieved a bowl, spoon and a box of shredded wheat from the kitchen cabinets.

Deanie slid down into one of the oak chairs at the table. Shaking her head in puzzlement, she snorted. "Hmph. I've heard it all now. You're actually looking forward to helping Rick paint a house? You, Lori Lee Guy, the girl who whines if she chips a fingernail. The girl who won't run to the grocery store without putting on her makeup and fixing her hair. The girl who washes her hands a dozen times a day because she can't stand for them to be dirty?''

Lori Lee prepared her cereal, then sat down and began eating hurriedly. "I figure that working together on something as aggravating as painting a house is a good test for our relationship." She munched several more bites, then jumped up and emptied the remainder of her food into the garbage disposal. "If Rick and I can spend the whole day together without wanting to kill each other, then maybe—"

"You are out of your mind," Deanie said. "I think your brain has short-circuited or something."

Loud knocking at the back door gained both women's immediate attention, and they glanced in the direction of the sound. Rick Warrick stood just outside, peeping in through the glass panes.

Lori Lee ran to the door, opened it and grabbed Rick's hand. "Come on in for a minute and say hello to Deanie. She stopped by on her way to the mall. I'm all ready to go." She led Rick inside the kitchen. "I packed lunch for us. I thought you and Darcie and I could have a backyard picnic."

"Hello, Rick," Deanie said. "She's packed enough food for Eve's whole family, too, so be careful not to throw your back out when you lift that basket."

Rick chuckled. "I'll be careful." He slipped his arm around Lori Lee's waist. "I hate to rush you, honey, but we need to get going. And I think I should warn you that we're going to have three little helpers today. Eve's boys and Darcie have white painter's caps on and brushes in their hands."

"Oh, how I envy y'all," Deanie said sarcastically. "If I weren't on my way to a day of misery shopping the sales at the mall, I'd come along and help."

"The more the merrier," Rick said. "It looks like with all the help I already have, this job could take a lot longer to finish than I originally thought."

"Well, don't let me keep y'all." Standing, Deanie glanced at Rick's arm holding Lori Lee close to his side.

"I've done what I came by to do." She checked her slacks pocket for her car keys.

The three walked out the back door together, Rick carrying the heavy, food-filled basket in one hand and possessively clasping Lori Lee's waist with the other.

Deanie opened the driver's door of her black Pontiac Bonneville, then turned and waved. "Well, don't have too much fun today. If I hear of any homicides in Tuscumbia, I'll know one of you murdered the other."

"Don't buy out the stores." Lori Lee waved goodbye as Rick helped her into his pickup.

He placed the picnic basket in the truck bed, hopped in the cab and backed his pickup out into the gravel alley. "I wanted to kiss you this morning, but when I found Deanie in your kitchen, I thought I'd better wait." Putting the truck in park, he reached over and pulled Lori Lee into his arms.

Sighing, she closed her eyes and lifted her arms around his neck. They kissed, their lips devouring, their tongues mating, and when they finally pulled apart, they were both breathless.

"You look sexy as hell in those old clothes," he told her, caressing her hip.

"Flattery will get you whatever you want, you know."

"If only that were true, I'd be spending the whole day in bed making love to you instead of painting Eve's house and baby-sitting three kids." Slipping his hand under her shirt, he covered her breast and squeezed gently.

She jerked on his wrist, pulling his hand away from her body. "Rick! Someone might see us."

"So?" Snapping around, he faced the windshield and clutched the steering wheel. "This being celibate is hard on a man." He peeked at her out of the corner of his eye. His lips twitched with a restrained smile.

Lori Lee laid her hand over his belt buckle, then playfully waltzed her fingers up and down his zipper. He sucked in his breath. She cupped him through his jeans. "Very hard," she said, then removed her tormenting hand.

"Woman, you're going to be the death of me." Gripping the steering wheel with white-knuckled ferocity, he knocked the gear into drive and revved the engine.

Lori Lee loved the way Rick kidded her, the way he made talking about sex so easy. He was an uninhibited man who was helping her tear down the restrictive walls she'd built around her life. With him, she felt free and just a little naughty. And when they made love, she was every bit as wild as he was.

Smiling, Lori Lee sat beside Rick as they drove through downtown Tuscumbia and up Sixth Street. As they passed Barber's Appliances, Lori Lee waved at Mindy Jenkins who was putting packages in the trunk of her car.

"I've got something I want to tell you," Rick said just as they passed the old post office building. "I'm going Monday to apply for a loan at Colbert Federal. That's where Bobo has always done business. I should know something one way or another within a week, maybe before your big spring recital."

"You'll get the loan," Lori Lee assured him. "Then Lewis Heating and Air-Conditioning will be all yours."

"God, I hope so. My whole future depends on getting that loan."

"Are you going to change the name once you're the boss? I think Warrick Heating and Air-Conditioning has a nice ring to it, don't you?"

"Yeah, I like the sound of that. Warrick Heating and Air-Conditioning." Rick grinned, thinking about how close he was to achieving his dream of owning his own business. "Who knows, maybe one of these days it'll be Warrick and Sons Heating and Air-Conditioning, or even Warrick and Daughters, if all my kids turn out to be girls."

The sun went behind the clouds, casting gray shadows on the earth. Even though the truck cab was toasty warm, a chill shivered through Lori Lee. All the color drained from her face and a wave of nausea rose in her stomach. *All my kids.* She heard Rick's words replaying over and over again in her mind. She shouldn't let what he'd said upset her. After all, she'd already known Rick wanted more children when he remarried. Maybe the wisest thing for her to do was be honest with him now, before their relationship became more serious. If there was even the slightest chance that marriage was in their future, Rick had a right to know she could never give him the children he wanted.

But there would be time enough to bare her soul to Rick, to open the unhealed wounds of her heart and tell him her deepest, darkest secret. It wasn't as if he'd said that he loved her. It wasn't as if he'd asked her to marry him.

If and when the day came that their relationship grew into something more than a sexual one—the way they both hoped—then she would tell him. But not today, not when they were both so happy and their lives filled with promise. Today she would enjoy sharing every moment with the man she loved. Tomorrow she would worry about losing him when he found out the truth.

Recital night was always a madhouse. Even though Lori Lee was the most organized person on earth and had everything perfectly planned down to the last detail, unexpected problems and minor emergencies seemed to be par for the course. Someone misplaced a baton. Someone else forgot their gold tights. Another got last-minute stage fright. And at least one mother had hysterics.

Lori Lee had realized several years ago, after her first Dixie Twirlers' recital, that without Aunt Birdie's assistance and the cooperation of her students' parents, she wouldn't have been able to pull off such an elaborate production so smoothly.

While Lori Lee announced the events and introduced the students performing in each upcoming act, Aunt Birdie oversaw the girls and their mothers. With several costume changes, equipment to be moved, props to be placed and the correct music set to play, one small oversight could easily ruin a production number.

The Deshler gymnasium was packed with parents, relatives and friends, each person expecting their little twirler to be the star performer. The humming roar of their voices drowned out all but the loudest noises, and the body heat generated by the crowd raised the inside temperature by a good ten degrees. Lori Lee was thankful that this April Saturday night had turned out to be a bit chilly.

Rick had presented both her and Darcie with a yellow rose before the recital began, and during each of Darcie's group performances, Lori Lee had searched the sea of faces and focused momentarily on Rick. In her heart, for the briefest of moments, she and Rick truly shared his daughter.

During intermission, Lori Lee went into the dressing rooms to congratulate her students and give encouragement to those she felt needed it. She paused when she walked past Darcie, reached out and caressed the child's plump cheek. Darcie beamed with happiness.

Lori Lee spoke softly, her voice a mere whisper, mouthing the words more than speaking them. "You were wonderful."

Standing several yards away, in the center of a group of mothers and daughters, Mara Royce complained. "I, for one, am opposed to any child receiving preferential treatment."

"Unless that child is her Steffie," Deanie Webber said quietly when she placed her hand on Lori Lee's shoulder. "Mrs. *Dr.* Royce is upset that Steffie wasn't given a solo number for the recital."

"Steffie's not ready for a solo number, and if she doesn't practice more, she never will be. What I'd like to do is tell Mara to withdraw Steffie from twirlers, but that wouldn't be fair to Steffie. Being part of my twirlers may be the only opportunity the child has to be treated like everyone else."

Mara raised her voice, speaking loud enough for everyone in the dressing rooms area to hear her. "I believe tonight's trophies should be awarded on merit alone, and for no other reason. I shall be greatly upset if anyone receives a trophy for any personal reasons.''

"Well, she's warned you, hasn't she?" Deanie patted Lori Lee on the back. "I know Darcie will receive a trophy because she's talented and has shown remarkable improvement in the three months since she took her first lesson, but Mara will try to convince everyone that your relationship with Rick is the reason."

"Let her do whatever she feels she has to do," Lori Lee said. "If Mara pushes me too far, she just might regret it."

"Well, well. I believe Aunt Birdie has finally rubbed off on you," Deanie said. "I've always admired that woman's ability to thumb her nose at the whole town and still have them kowtowing to her like she was a queen."

"Besides simply not giving a damn what people think of her, Aunt Birdie possess complete confidence in who she is. People around here respect two things she possesses. The ten million dollars she inherited from her last husband and her old Southern lineage. All four of Aunt Birdie's great-grandfathers were Confederate soldiers, you know."

"Did someone mention my name?" Carrying a huge bouquet of red roses, Birdie pushed her way into the dressing area, her wide hips brushing several little girls' shoulders as she passed them.

"What have you got there, Aunt Birdie?" Deanie asked.

"Flowers for Lori Lee. They just arrived." Birdie handed Lori Lee the card, then tossed the bouquet into a nearby chair. "They're from Powell. I took the liberty of seeing who they were from." Birdie handed her niece the white card she held.

Lori Lee read the message silently. *Couldn't let your big night go by without wishing you all the best. When you come to your senses, call me. I'll be waiting. Love, Powell.* She handed the card to Deanie, who scanned it quickly.

"Sure of himself, isn't he?" Deanie commented.

"Too damned sure, if you ask me," Birdie said.

"I don't have time to worry about Powell right now."

Lori Lee glanced at the red roses, then lifted her hand to her hair and caressed Rick's yellow rose that she'd placed behind her ear. "Intermission is almost over." She clapped her hands. "Let's get moving, girls. We've got an appreciative audience waiting for us."

The trophies, which varied in size from six inches to two feet, covered two large tables that had been placed against the wall, behind the loudspeaker podium. Most of the fathers, including Rick, climbed down from the bleachers and aimed their video equipment. Rick had told Lori Lee that he planned to borrow Tom Nelson's camera.

Grandparents squirmed in their seats. Mothers wrung their hands and uttered silent prayers. The girls, dressed in their pink-and-white Dixie Twirlers uniforms, circled the gym.

One by one Lori Lee announced the winners, and with each presentation came thundering applause. Everyone attending expected this phase of the recital to take extra time. Each child's award was of equal importance to her and her family.

"And this year's award for Best First-Year Student goes to—" Lori Lee paused long enough to focus momentarily on Rick's face "—Darcie Warrick."

Even with the distance between them, Lori Lee saw the sheen of moisture in Rick's eyes. Or perhaps she just sensed it. Regardless, she knew, perhaps better than anyone, how much seeing his daughter win this award meant to him.

Hesitant applause mingled with questioning murmurs. Darcie marched forward. With tears streaming down her sweet face, she reached out and accepted the shiny, twelve-inch-high golden trophy with her name printed in large letters across the front.

Eve and Tom Nelson stood and clapped louder and harder than anyone, except Aunt Birdie. Trey and Mark jumped up and down, whooping and hollering. Rick zeroed the video camera in on Darcie. When Deanie and Phil Webber stood and continued clapping, several other parents joined them, and within a couple of minutes most of the parents were applauding Darcie's win.

Mara Royce sat rigidly, her back straight as a stick. Crossing her arms over her chest and puckering her mouth, she glared at Lori Lee.

The moment the awards presentation ended and Lori Lee thanked everyone for coming to the recital, the crowd dispersed. Children ran wild all over the gym, proudly holding up their trophies. Mara Royce made a beeline to Lori Lee.

"Here she comes," Birdie said. "Brace yourself, niece. Now's the time to show what you're made of."

Lori Lee barely had time to walk out from behind the speaker's podium before Mara confronted her. "If you think for one minute that I'm going to let you get away with what you did tonight, then you'd better think again," Mara yelled loud enough to be heard in the next county.

Lori Lee glanced over Mara's shoulder and saw the Nelsons and the Webbers following Rick across the gym. They were all headed straight toward her. Quite a few other parents delayed their exit, obviously waiting around to see what was going to happen.

"Aunt Birdie, please make sure Darcie gathers up all of her things from the dressing room," Lori Lee said.

"Don't you worry. I'll make sure Darcie's kept busy until this is over." Birdie scurried across the gym, but before she could reach Darcie, Rick grabbed his daughter's hand and brought her across the gym with him.

Lori Lee faced Mara. "I don't think this is the time or place to discuss any complaints you have. Not with so many of the girls still here."

"What's the matter?" Mara asked mockingly. "Are you afraid your precious little Darcie might find out the real reason she won her trophy?"

"Mara, if you have one shred of decency in you, don't make a scene in front of these children."

"If you are really so concerned about your students, why would you risk ruining your reputation and shaming the Dixie Twirlers?" Mara pointed her finger in Lori Lee's face. "People know you're having an affair with that no-good Rick Warrick, and in order to keep him happy, you're lavishing a lot of attention on his daughter. The only reason Darcie Warrick received the Best First-Year Student trophy instead of Steffie is because you're sleeping with her father. He must really be something in bed for you to jeopardize—"

Three things happened simultaneously. Darcie Warrick asked her father if what Mrs. Royce said was true, that she received her trophy because he was Lori Lee's boyfriend. Rick snatched the trophy out of his daughter's arms while she was still talking. And Lori Lee Guy slapped Mara so hard that she left a red-stained image of her handprint on Mara's cheek.

Crying out in pain, Mara stared at Lori Lee in disbelief.

"Ohmigod!" The moment Deanie Webber groaned the slurred words aloud, silence fell over the gymnasium and the onlookers froze as her voice rang out loud and clear.

Rick shoved the shiny trophy into Mara's arms. She stared up at Rick, her teary eyes wide with fear. She clutched the trophy in her trembling hands.

"Take the damn thing if it means so much to you. Take it and r—" Clenching his teeth tightly together, Rick snorted. "And to think I wanted my daughter to associate with your kind, to fit in with your child's group of friends."

"Rick." Lori Lee reached out for him, but hesitated when he glared at her, anger and bitterness in his eyes.

"As far as I'm concerned, the whole bunch of you can go straight to hell and take all the stupid trophies with you." Rick lifted Darcie onto his hip. "Y'all know damn well that Lori Lee isn't the type of woman to play favorites when it comes to giving out awards to these kids. My Darcie won that trophy—" he nodded his head sharply at the trophy Mara Royce clutched to her bosom "—because of her talent, and for no other reason."

"Everybody knows that," Aunt Birdie shouted. "Even Mara knows, but she's too jealous-hearted to face the truth."

Rick turned around and carried a sobbing Darcie out of the gym. The Nelson family hurried after him.

Lori Lee felt as if her whole life had suddenly ended, as if the world ceased to exist. Her body was numb, her mind swirling, her emotions completely haywire.

Everyone in the gym stood silently, watching and waiting. Mara tilted her pug nose into the air, twisted her short neck toward her shoulder and stared at the crowd. "I'm not the one at fault. She is." Mara pointed her finger at Lori Lee.

No one said a word. Lori Lee reached over and jerked Darcie's trophy out of Mara's clutches. "This isn't Steffie's. She received the trophy she deserved. This one belongs to Darcie Warrick because her talent and hard work earned it for her."

Mara glowered at Lori Lee. "You've let your infatuation for that white trash Romeo—"

"Don't you dare say another word," Lori Lee warned her, then turned and looked out at the crowd, many of them Tuscumbia's elite. "Rick Warrick is a good man, who loves his daughter and has done everything he possibly can to earn the respect and acceptance of this town. All he wants is to make a place here for himself and his child. But y'all won't give him a chance, won't forget who he used to be or forgive him for sins he committed when he was just a boy."

"She doesn't see the man for what he is." Mara pleaded her case to the stunned audience. "If she wasn't so infatuated with him, she'd know what we know. That A. K. Warrick came from nothing and that's what he still is. Nothing."

"I'm not infatuated with Rick," Lori Lee said, her voice deceptively calm. "I'm in love with him."

A cumulative gasp came from the crowd. Aunt Birdie grinned. Deanie bit her bottom lip. Mara Royce smirked, as if saying, See, I was right all along.

Lori Lee felt an enormous sense of relief well up and overflow inside her. Finally, she had admitted the secret her heart had kept hidden, even from her, and the joy of that revelation spread quickly through her mind and body.

"I love Rick Warrick." She spoke the words, testing them, liking the sound of them on her lips. "Did you hear me? I love Rick Warrick. And I love his daughter. But I don't think anyone here truly believes that I'm the kind of person who would award any child a trophy she didn't deserve."

"Hear, hear," Birdie Pierpont said.

Grasping Darcie's trophy tightly in her hand and not acknowledging anyone's attempts to speak to her, Lori Lee made her way through the murmuring crowd.

"Lori Lee," Deanie called out and started to go after her.

Birdie grabbed Deanie's wrist. "She'll be all right."

"She's upset. She doesn't need to be alone," Deanie said.

"She won't be alone." Birdie smiled. "If I know my niece, she's on her way over to see Rick and Darcie."

"Oh." Deanie nodded agreement. "You're probably right."

Lori Lee parked her Riviera in the driveway behind the Nelsons' Bronco. Glancing up when she got out, she noticed the lights were on in the garage apartment. She wasn't sure what kind of reception she'd receive, but regardless of whether or not Rick wanted her here, she wasn't going to leave until she had given Darcie the trophy that rightfully belonged to her.

Now wasn't the time to confess her undying love to Rick.

There would be time enough for the two of them to work through their problems later. Right now, her main concern was Darcie. She couldn't bear the thought of that special little girl suffering because of Mara Royce's sick jealousy.

Lori Lee climbed the steps to Rick's apartment, hesitated momentarily on the stoop, then took a deep breath and knocked. She waited. And she waited. She knocked again.

"Whoever it is, leave us the hell alone," Rick bellowed.

"Rick, it's Lori Lee. Please, let me come in. I want to see Darcie." She clutched the trophy in her hand.

"Go away."

"I'm not leaving until I see Darcie."

Rick jerked open the door and glared at Lori Lee, then glanced down at the trophy in her hand. "Don't you think you've done enough for my daughter? She's in her room right now, crying her eyes out. She keeps asking me over and over again if she really didn't win the award for Best First-Year Student."

"Well, I hope you told her that she most certainly won the award and that Mara Royce is a mean, vindictive, jealous-hearted woman and no one believed a word she said."

"Do you honestly think no one believed her?" Rick asked cynically.

"No one who really mattered." Lori Lee laid her hand on his forearm, longing to embrace him and tell him that she loved him.

Rick yanked back his arm. "Go home. Please. Leave us alone. I can't deal with anything else tonight. I've had just about all I can stand."

"No, Daddy, don't send Lori Lee away," Darcie cried out as she came running from her bedroom and through the living room. She shoved on Rick's legs, prompting him to move over so that she could get past him.

Kneeling when Darcie ran toward her, Lori Lee shoved the trophy into Rick's hand and swooped his child up into her arms. Darcie flung her arms around Lori Lee's neck, hugging tightly.

"Don't go, please. Stay with me," Darcie begged.

Rick clenched his teeth as emotions he could barely control rose in his throat, threatening to choke him. Moisture misted his vision. He swallowed hard, trying desperately not to give in to his feelings. It broke his heart to see how much his daughter loved Lori Lee.

He'd been a fool to think this woman, this beautiful, perfect woman, could ever belong to him. Could ever be a part of his and Darcie's life. Surely after what had happened tonight, she realized it, too. Mara Royce had not only broken Darcie's heart, she had humiliated Lori Lee by announcing her affair with him to the twirler parents. It had been one thing for people to speculate about their relationship, but it was another to have their affair publicly denounced by one of the town's social grande dames.

How the hell would sweet, ladylike, Southern belle Lori Lee ever live down having slapped Mara Royce in front of a large portion of Tuscumbia's population?

Stroking Darcie's back tenderly, Lori Lee glanced at Rick, then took a step toward him. He backed up and out of the way, allowing her to bring his daughter into the apartment. Lori Lee carried Darcie into her room and sat down on the bed, putting Darcie on her lap. Rick slammed the front door. Following them, he stood in the doorway and watched while Darcie laid her head on Lori Lee's shoulder and Lori Lee kissed Darcie on the forehead.

"Mrs. Royce wanted Steffie to win the award for Best First-Year Student." Lori Lee took Darcie's hand in hers. "Sometimes grown-ups can be very selfish and cruel. They can do and say things that hurt other people when they become so jealous they can't think straight."

"Mrs. Royce said that you gave me the award 'cause you and Daddy sleep together," Darcie said. "I'm not sure what that means, except that you're Daddy's girlfriend."

"Yes, sweetheart, I'm your daddy's girlfriend, but I didn't give you the award for that reason. And I love you so much, Darcie. You're very special to me. But I didn't give you the award for that reason, either.''

"Then why did you give me the award?"

Darcie looked up at Lori Lee with eyes an identical blue to her own. Lori Lee's breath caught in her throat and for a brief moment she couldn't speak.

"You know the reason why," Lori Lee said. "Don't you?"

Darcie sat straight up and looked Lori Lee directly in the eye. "You gave me the award because I really am the best first-year student."

"And that's the only reason." Lori Lee embraced Rick's daughter, the little girl she desperately wanted to be hers.

Rick cleared his throat. Two pairs of big, blue eyes stared at him. "I think I have something that belongs to you, Miss Warrick." He walked into the room and handed the trophy to Darcie.

She hugged it to her chest. "It's really mine." She looked to Lori Lee for affirmation.

"Yes, it's really yours. You deserve it. You earned it." Lori Lee slid Darcie off her lap and onto the bed. "It's past your bedtime, young lady. You've had a big night, in more ways than one. I think it's time for you to go to sleep. Where's your pajamas?"

"Hanging on a peg in the bathroom," Darcie said.

"Then you go get into them and I'll tuck you in bed before I leave," Lori Lee told the child.

"Would you read me a bedtime story first?"

Lori Lee glanced at Rick. He nodded an agreement to his daughter's request. "Do you have a copy of *Beauty and the Beast?*" she asked.

"Get my *Beauty and the Beast* book for her, Daddy, while I go put on my pajamas." With her trophy clutched to her chest, Darcie jumped out of bed and rushed toward the bathroom.

Rick pulled a book from the stack on a bottom shelf of Darcie's nightstand and handed it to Lori Lee. "Thanks for being so good to her. You mean a lot to her, you know. Probably too much."

"I love Darcie," Lori Lee confessed aloud, and silently added, *And I love you, too, Rick. With all my heart.*

"Yeah, I see that you do. It won't be easy for any of us, but I think it's best if I take Darcie out of your dance and baton classes. All the other kids will shun her after what happened tonight."

"I think you're wrong about that." Opening the book, she glanced at it and then laid it on the bed. "I may lose one or two students, besides Steffie Royce, because of what Mara said tonight, but I have a lot more faith in my friends and acquaintances than you do. Why don't you give the people of Tuscumbia what you say you want from them? Give them a chance to prove themselves to you. Believe me, Rick, only a handful of our citizens are true snobs."

"Damn, I'd like to think you're right. I just don't know. I don't want to see Darcie hurt again. Not ever."

"Neither do I. I promise you that—"

"I'm all ready for bed." Darcie came flying into the room, her little hand circling the base of her trophy.

Rick lifted her up and into her bed, then leaned over and kissed her. "Is it all right with you two girls if I hang around and listen to the story?"

"If it's all right with Lori Lee, it's all right with me."

"I have no objections."

"Okay, Daddy, you can stay."

"Why don't you put your trophy on the nightstand?" Lori Lee suggested.

Darcie set her trophy on the nightstand, petted it lovingly, then cuddled against Lori Lee. In less than ten minutes, just as Lori Lee reached the part in the story where Belle had thrown herself on her bed and was sobbing, Darcie fell sound asleep. Lori Lee read on for a couple of minutes, then closed the book, leaned over and placed it back on top of the stack on the nightstand shelf.

When she started to get up, Rick offered her his hand.

She accepted his assistance, smiling at him and whispering her thanks. She gasped when he suddenly pulled her into his arms.

"Rick?"

"I'll walk you to your car." He looked at her as if he wanted to kiss her, but instead he released her.

"All right."

When they reached the bottom of the stairs outside, Rick took Lori Lee's hand in his and squeezed. She stood perfectly still. Her heartbeat thundered in her ears. Her pulse raced at breakneck speed.

"I don't want to let you go, honey."

"You know I can't stay." She threaded her fingers through his. "I can't...we can't...not with Darcie—"

Rick dragged her toward the garage. Startled by his actions, she hesitated, stumbling against him when he forced her into sudden movement. Rick yanked open a side door to the garage and pulled Lori Lee into the dark interior.

"Have you ever made out in a truck?" he asked.

"No."

"Would you like to?" He nuzzled her neck.

"Yes," she said breathlessly.

Nine

Rick slammed the door shut with his foot, closing them inside the cool, quiet darkness. The shimmery moonlight shone through the lone window at the back side of the garage, casting murky shadows across the old blue pickup. Lori Lee could barely make out Rick's facial features, but she had no trouble feeling him. He pressed her against the wall, his big body hard, straining and rigidly intent. Lifting her arms, he manacled both of her wrists in his huge hand and held them over her head.

Unable to embrace him, to touch his chest or shoulders, she whimpered as sensual need throbbed in her feminine core. She leaned into him, rubbing herself intimately against him.

"You want it as bad as I do, don't you, honey?" He mouthed the words against her neck. "These weeks of celibacy have made you crazy, haven't they? As crazy as I am."

"Rick. Rick. Please." She had known love and desire

and sexual pleasure before, but nothing had prepared her for the fiery, raging hunger Rick Warrick ignited in her every time he looked at her. She had never known this aching need to have a man buried deep inside her, had never experienced the overwhelming kind of lust that ruled her mind and body.

While he held her wrists captive, he slid his other hand behind her back and jerked down the zipper of her black crepe dress. He unhooked her black lace bra. She leaned the back of her head against the wall and gasped for air as he released her hands, dragged her dress to her hips and yanked her bra down her arms, then grabbed her arms again. He tossed her bra onto the floor, then lowered his mouth and laved one puckered nipple. She moaned. Rick raised his head.

"Your breasts cry out for my mouth, baby. You love it when I do this—" he licked one nipple and then the other "—don't you?" He savored the mewing sounds she made as he continued tormenting her, taking turns licking and sucking until she writhed against him, lifting one of her legs and rubbing it up and down his.

He bumped his sex into her aching femininity, grinding into her with hard, circular pressure. "Is this what you want?"

She couldn't think, couldn't breathe. She could only feel.

"Answer me, baby," he demanded, his voice husky with sexual need. "Tell me you like my mouth on your breasts. Tell me you want me inside you, filling you completely."

"Rick. Oh, Rick, yes," she whispered, her body trembling as painful need urged her to fight his hold on her wrists.

When she struggled to free herself, wanting to grab him and hold him close, to run her hands over his chest and rip his clothes from his body, Rick tightened his grip, refusing to release her.

"Do you want to touch me?" he asked her teasingly. "Tell me what I want to hear and I'll let you touch me."

"I—I like your mouth..." Shuddering with aching pleasure, she cried out when he pinched her nipple. "I like your mouth on my breasts." The words rushed out of her. "And I want you. Oh, Rick, I want you so."

He tugged her dress and lace half-slip down and over her hips. The soft crepe and slinky silk pooled around her ankles like obsidian clouds.

He cupped her intimately, then slipped a couple of fingers inside her black lace bikini panties. She gasped the moment his fingers made contact with her throbbing little nub.

"You're right on the edge, aren't you, baby? It wouldn't take much to send you over." He inserted his fingers into her damp, hot body. She squeezed her legs shut, trapping his hand between her thighs. "Tell me exactly what you want. Tell me what it's going to take to put you out of your misery."

"Make love to me," she pleaded. "I want you inside me. I ache for you."

The moment he released her wrists, he scooped her up in his arms and carried her to the truck. She kicked off her black leather heels, then grabbed his face, spearing her fingers into his hair, kissing him again and again. Rick unhitched the truck's tailgate and lifted Lori Lee up on the edge. She shivered when her hips and legs made contact with the cold metal.

Clenching fistfuls of his tailored blue shirt, she jerked him forward, then she popped several buttons off his shirt as she ripped it open. Spreading her hands over his chest, she sighed, loving the feel of his hair-covered muscles.

"You want me bad, don't you, baby?" Rick unbuckled his belt, unzipped his khaki slacks and hurriedly pulled them down his legs. When they caught on his shoes, he yanked his dress slippers and socks off along with his pants. "Don't worry, I'm here. And I'm going to give you what you need. What we both need."

He tore her sheer panty hose in his haste to remove them

and her lace panties. Her trembling hands yanked his briefs
down over his hips. Hot, moist and naked, Lori Lee opened
her legs in an invitation he could not refuse. He lifted her
hips as he stepped between her legs and pulled her to the
very edge of the truck's unfolded tailgate.

"You're mine," he said when he gripped her buttocks
and thrust hard and heavy into her, burying himself deeply.

"I'm yours...yours...yours..." She clung to him, ac-
cepting his wild lunges, loving the feel of Rick filling her
completely.

Their coupling was fast and furious. Rick's big, hairy
body dampened with sweat as he drove into her repeatedly,
bumping her hips up and down and bouncing her breasts.
Lori Lee sheathed him like a glove, clutching him with hot,
wet fury.

"Good. So good, baby," he told her seconds before he
felt her tighten around him. Her body shook as the power
and pleasure of satisfaction burst inside her.

Moaning with intense pleasure, Lori Lee dug her nails
into his buttocks, then whispered passionate, earthy words
of inducement. The feel of her quivering, encompassing
heat and the insistence of her seductive, verbal demands
hurled him into oblivion. His release hit him with violent
force. Giving out a long, guttural cry of fulfillment, he buried his face between her breasts. She lifted his chin and
looked at him adoringly.

"I love you, Rick."

Groaning, he shut his eyes. "Oh, Lori Lee."

He had wanted her for as long as he could remember,
had fantasized about making love to her, of claiming her
as his own. But never in his wildest dreams had he ever
thought she would love him.

He took her mouth savagely, possessively, and felt himself growing hard once again. "I can't get enough of you,
baby."

Reluctantly pulling out of her body, Rick lifted her in
his arms and carried her around the truck, then opened the

driver's door and set her on the seat. He climbed in beside her and pulled her into his arms. "No more celibacy," he told her. "From now on, while we're dating, we're going to make love. Every day. Even if I have to come to you in the middle of the night."

"Every day," she agreed, then wrapped her arms around his neck and dragged him down on top of her as she lay on the seat.

He hadn't told her that he loved her, too. She had so desperately wanted to hear him say the words. Perhaps he didn't love her. Or maybe he just wasn't ready to tell her. She could be patient. She could wait. She knew that he would never lie to her, never pretend, never profess to love her if he didn't.

"Lori Lee, honey, are you sure you really love me?" he asked, his sex pulsating against her belly. "Sometimes people confuse good sex with love."

"I love you," she said. "I love the sex, too, of course." She eased her thighs apart slowly and lifted her hips.

"Dammit, woman, you're driving me crazy." He plunged into her, gasping with pleasure as her body welcomed him.

"It's all right if you can't tell me that you love me," she whispered in his ear as he once again claimed her with pure, raw passion. "This is enough. For now."

Clutching the telephone in his hand, Rick stared at it as if it were an alien being. Then, when his mind absorbed the reality of his recently completed conversation, he slammed the receiver onto the wall base.

"Dammit! Dammit!" He kicked his booted toe against the doorpost and beat his fist against the closed kitchen door.

"You didn't get the loan." Eve dropped the knife she was using to spread mayonnaise on their sandwiches, wiped her hands on the towel draped across her shoulder and rushed over to her brother.

When she tried to put her hand on his shoulder, he jerked away, turning his back to her. He didn't want Eve to see him on the verge of crying. Before he faced her, he had to get his emotions under control. He was so angry that it wouldn't take much to push him over the edge. If he could get his hands around Mara Royce's short, plump neck right now, he'd strangle the life out of her.

"I'm sorry, Eve. Just give me a minute. Okay?"

Taking several steps away from Rick, she stood in the middle of her immaculately clean white-and-hunter-green kitchen. "What did Mr. Percy say? Did he give you a reason for turning down your loan application?"

Taking a deep, semicalming breath, Rick grunted. "Oh, yeah, he gave me a reason all right. It seems my application was given special consideration. Colbert Federal's president reviewed it, and Mr. John Hobart himself decided I wasn't a good risk."

"John Hobart," Eve repeated the name. "But that's—"

"Mara Royce's father." Rick turned to face his sister.

"Oh, that horrible woman. She actually involved her father in her petty little scheme for revenge." Eve threw up her hands in a sign of disgust. "There has to be something we can do. We'll hire a lawyer. We'll sue Colbert Federal. We'll sue Mara Royce!"

"If I thought it would do any good, I'd go to Birmingham and hire the best attorney I could afford," Rick said. "But there would be no way to prove a thing, little sister. It's Hobart's bank, and if he says I'm a poor loan risk, then my bet is he can find a way to back up his claim."

"Colbert Federal isn't the only bank around here," Eve reminded him. "You can apply for a loan at another bank."

"Yeah, well, Mr. Percy advised me against doing that."

"What do you mean? Did he threaten you?"

"Not exactly." Rick walked over and put his arm around Eve's shoulder. "He simply commented that he was sure I'd find similar problems with other local banks, and that Mr. Hobart suggested that before I tried reapplying anywhere else I might want to get advice from a lawyer. He recommended Powell Goodman.''

"It's a conspiracy. That's what it is. Mara Royce and Powell Goodman are out to get you.'' Eve hugged Rick, then pulled away from him. "Well, they're not going to get away with it.''

"Look, sis, I've known all along that it wasn't going to be easy to make a place for me and Darcie in Tuscumbia. I was aware of the risk I was taking, counting on the people around here to give me a chance.''

"Most people have given you a chance,'' Eve told him. "Powell Goodman and Mara Royce are a small minority.''

"Yeah, but they're a powerful, dangerous minority.''

His gut instincts had told him that something would mess up his dreams, now that they were within his reach. He'd been too damn lucky. His sister and brother-in-law had bent over backward to help him, even giving him and Darcie a place to live. And by some miracle, Lori Lee Guy had fallen in love with him—something he'd never dreamed possible. To make things perfect, Darcie and Lori Lee adored each other. He had figured that, once this loan went through and he'd bought Bobo's business, he just might propose to Lori Lee.

Now what the hell was he going to do? Even at best, he had little to offer her. Just himself and Darcie. And his solemn vow to be a good, faithful husband until the day he died. But now, he couldn't go to her, a complete failure, and ask her to endure the town's ridicule.

"Rick, don't give up. There's a solution to this problem, if we can just find it.''

"Yeah, sure,'' Rick said. "I don't know how I'm going to tell Lori Lee. She's suffered enough in the past few days because of me. After that stunt Mara Royce pulled at the recital Saturday night, I wouldn't have blamed Lori Lee if she'd never wanted to see me again.''

"When are you going to get it through that thick head of yours that Lori Lee Guy loves you?''

"I can't figure out why. What the hell does a woman like that see in a guy like me?"

"I've asked myself that same question," Eve said jokingly. "Why don't you ask Lori Lee?"

"What I should do, for her sake, is break off things right now." Rick couldn't bear the thought of losing Lori Lee, but he didn't have the right to drag her down with him, to ask her to share her life with a guy who didn't have a prayer of making it in this town.

"You're talking as if everything is hopeless when it's not." Eve returned to the task of preparing sandwiches, quickly putting together two ham-and-cheese combinations. "Sit down and eat and we'll discuss the possibilities."

"Just put mine on a paper towel and I'll eat it on the way back to work. My lunch hour is nearly over."

Eve tore off a paper towel, wrapped it around one of the sandwiches and handed it to Rick. "Here. And don't do anything stupid, like breaking up with Lori Lee out of some misplaced sense of chivalry. I promise you that I'll find a way for you to get a loan."

Rick grabbed the sandwich in one hand, then cupped his sister's chin, lifting her face for a quick kiss. "My little miracle worker."

"It won't take a miracle."

"Yes, it will, sis. Happiness just isn't in the cards for a guy like me. I wasn't meant to be one of the lucky ones. The first time life kicked me on my rear, I should have stayed down instead of clawing my way back up time and time again."

"Oh, Rick," Eve said as Rick closed the door behind him. "It breaks my heart to hear you talk like that...."

Lori Lee answered the Sparkle and Shine shop's telephone on the second ring, identifying both herself and her business.

"Lori Lee, this is Eve Nelson."

"Hello, Eve. How are you?"

"I've been better."

Lori Lee's stomach tightened into knots. Something was wrong with Rick. Why else would Eve be calling her?

"What's the matter?" Lori Lee asked.

"Colbert Federal turned down Rick's loan," Eve said.

"Oh, no. I suppose he's angry and hurt and roaring like a wounded lion."

"You know our Rick."

Aunt Birdie, who was removing the Easter display from the show window, backed her ample behind out of the window and set her wide feet on the floor. "What happened to Rick?"

Lori Lee covered the phone's mouthpiece with her hand. "Rick didn't get his loan from Colbert Federal," she told her aunt.

"Look, Lori Lee," Eve said. "Rick's ready to give up, to call it quits with you and forget all of his dreams."

"There's more to this than you've told me, isn't there?" Lori Lee asked.

"Mr. Percy at Colbert Federal advised Rick not to seek a loan locally. It seems Mara Royce persuaded her father to reject Rick's loan application and Mr. Hobart and Powell Goodman have put the word out that Rick's a poor risk."

Lori Lee saw red. Literally. She shut her eyes tightly, allowing the anger inside her to build until she was on the verge of exploding. The sheer force of her rage rendered her momentarily speechless. Tears gathered in her eyes as pain consumed her.

"What on earth's wrong?" Birdie grabbed the phone away from Lori Lee, then clasped her niece's shoulder and gave her a sound shake. She placed the receiver to her ear. "Eve, Birdie Pierpont here. Lori Lee's so upset she's crying. Tell me what happened, and don't leave out a thing." Birdie listened while Eve explained the entire situation.

Lori Lee rubbed her throbbing temples as she tried to calm herself. She was not going to allow Mara Royce or Powell Goodman to hurt Rick. They had no right to take their jealous fury out on him, when she was the object of their irrational feelings. If it hadn't been for her, this wouldn't have happened. If Rick lost his dream, it would be her fault.

"Well, don't you worry, Eve," Birdie said. "I can take care of this problem with one phone call. A great deal of my money is scattered around several local banks, most of it in Tuscumbia Savings and Loan where my nephew, Guy Stephenson, works. You leave everything to me. I'll see to it that Rick gets his loan."

While Aunt Birdie continued chatting with Eve, Lori Lee saw Rick's old truck pull up in front of the shop. "Get off the phone, Aunt Birdie. Rick's here. He just parked. Now he's getting out."

"Calm down, sugar," Birdie told her niece as she held her hand over the phone's mouthpiece. "I've got things under control. You take Rick on back to the storeroom and convince him that Powell Goodman and John Hobart have no influence whatsoever over at Tuscumbia Savings and Loan. Talk him into applying for a loan there today."

"Today?"

"If he applies today, he'll get his loan tomorrow." Birdie uncovered the telephone mouthpiece and told Eve that she'd keep her posted, said goodbye and hung up the receiver.

"Oh, Aunt Birdie, you're wonderful!" Lori Lee wiped the tears from her eyes.

Rick opened the front door and walked in, a scowling look on his face that proclaimed to one and all that his life wasn't worth living.

"We've got to talk, honey." He grabbed Lori Lee's arm. "Somewhere private."

"Come on back to the storage room." Lori Lee glanced at her aunt. "Take care of things out here for me, please."

"I'll be glad to take care of everything," Birdie assured her.

Lori Lee led Rick into the storage room, closed the door

and wrapped her arms around him. Immediately, he prized her arms off him and held her shoulders, keeping their bodies from touching.

"What's wrong?" she asked.

"Things aren't going to work out," he said. "I was a fool to think you and I had a prayer of making things work. I'm a born loser. You're a golden princess. If I don't let you go now, I'm going to drag you down into the mire with me."

"You heard from Colbert Federal about your loan, didn't you?"

"Yeah, honey, it isn't good news."

"Colbert Federal isn't the only local bank."

"I've already had this conversation with my sister."

"Come over here and sit down, and tell me everything." She clasped his hand in hers and coaxed him over to the small table and chairs in the corner of the storage room.

He told her every detail of his conversation with Mr. Percy from Colbert Federal, leaving out nothing. She damned Mara Royce and Powell Goodman for the hateful, jealous-hearted creatures they were, then she told him that she wasn't going to allow anyone to ruin his dreams and destroy his and Darcie's future.

"There's one bank in town where neither Mara's daddy nor Powell have any influence," she told him. "Tuscumbia Savings and Loan. I think you should go over there right now and put in a loan application."

"Didn't you listen to a thing I said? Nobody in this town is going to loan me a dime."

"I'm sure Tuscumbia Savings and Loan will consider your application." When he shook his head and frowned, she reached out and laid her hand over his where it rested atop the table. "What have you got to lose? Give it a try. Do it for me. After all, I have a big stake in your success. If you can't buy Bobo's business, you're going to walk out of my life, and I can't let that happen."

Turning her hand over, he traced the faint lines in her palm. "You're a hopeless optimist, honey."

"And you're a cynic and a pessimist, and I love you."

"Did I happen to mention that you're also crazy?" A hint of a smile twitched his lips.

"Rick, we can't let this one setback destroy what we're trying to build together. A good life for you and Darcie, and maybe even a future for you and me."

"I'm never going to be good enough for you, honey. No matter what." Tugging on her hand, he urged her up and onto her feet, then drew her slowly into his arms. "You're perfect. Absolutely perfect. You can give a man everything, make all his dreams come true. You should love a man who can give you everything in return."

"Rick, I'm not perfect. There are things about me that you don't know, things I should have told you."

"I know everything about you that I need to know." He cupped her hips, easing her closer and closer, until their bodies touched intimately.

"You've told me about your shortcomings over and over again," Lori Lee said. "You keep telling me that I shouldn't love you because you're too much this and not enough that. How do I convince you that I love you despite your shortcomings? I can live with your imperfections, Rick. Can you live with mine?"

"You don't have any imperfections." He rubbed his cheek against hers. "You're the most perfect woman on earth."

"What if I did have a flaw, an imperfection that kept me from being all that you want me to be?"

"But you are all that I want you to be. No man could ask for more."

She knew she should tell him about her miscarriages, about her operation and her subsequent infertility. He had every right to know that his perfect woman was terribly flawed. Her perfect body wasn't capable of performing a woman's most basic function. Conceiving, carrying and giving birth to a child.

And she *would* tell him. Once he'd applied for and received a loan from Tuscumbia Savings and Loan, she would be completely honest with him. Before he asked her to marry him. Before he committed himself. She didn't want Rick unless he truly loved her, completely and unconditionally, as she loved him. And she realized that once he discovered just how imperfect she was, he might not even want her.

Ten

Rick had never owned a suit in his entire life, not until now. And he didn't think he'd ever get used to wearing a tie. The damn thing felt like a noose around his big neck. But today was special—it was a day that required him to look like a successful businessman.

Three weeks ago he'd just about given up hope of ever realizing his dreams, and now here he was at a party given in his honor to celebrate the reopening, under a new name, of his own heating and air-conditioning company. Eve had insisted on a ribbon-cutting ceremony earlier today, and Aunt Birdie and Lori Lee had helped her plan tonight's party.

Not only had Lori Lee been a hundred percent right about Tuscumbia Savings and Loan approving his loan application, but she'd been right about the majority of her friends and acquaintances, most of whom were milling around in Eve's home right now. Powell Goodman and the

Royces were conspicuous by their absence, but Rick figured nobody missed them. He sure as hell didn't.

He'd been amazed not only by how many fellow businessmen had attended today's ribbon-cutting ceremony, but that they had actually invited him to join several of their local business-related organizations. And at tonight's party, a Tuscumbia pharmacist and a restaurateur had invited him to play golf with them next Saturday. Golf? Rick Warrick playing golf? Aunt Birdie, who had overheard the conversation, had accepted for him and later told him he could borrow her late husband's set of clubs.

Lori Lee smiled at him from across the room, and the bottom dropped out of his stomach. Kneeling in front of Darcie, Lori Lee was retying the pink ribbon in his daughter's hair. And for the millionth time he marveled at the similarity between woman and child.

He was damn glad he'd been wrong about everything, that he wasn't destined to be a loser, that life was finally giving him a hand up instead of a kick in the pants. He had to be the luckiest guy on the face of the earth. Who else had so many people on his side, rooting for him, believing in him, refusing to let him give up when things looked hopeless? And what other reformed bad boy had the good fortune to have Lori Lee Guy in love with him?

He slipped his hand in his coat pocket, checking for the hundredth time to make sure the ring box was still there. Maybe he should have waited, given Lori Lee a chance to come to her senses and realize that he'd never be good enough for her. But while he was on a winning streak, he figured there was no time like the present to reach out and take what he'd always wanted.

He wished he could have bought her a big diamond, something she could show proudly to her friends. But he couldn't afford a big diamond, so he'd chosen something less expensive—a ring that reminded him of Lori Lee. The marquis-cut golden topaz lying in the jeweler's case had caught his eye the minute he'd walked into the store. The band was gold, the front and sides of it filigree, giving the ring an antique look, and the topaz was surrounded by tiny diamond chips. The topaz had been less expensive than the diamond he'd wanted to buy her, but even the topaz would have to be paid for in monthly installments. Right now, he was just about as broke as a guy could be.

Tonight, when he took Lori Lee home after the party, he planned to ask her to marry him. He'd be up front with her, remind her of all the reasons she'd be a fool to say yes, and then tell her he loved her and beg her to be his wife. Somehow he'd find a way to give her whatever her heart desired. More than anything he wanted to make Lori Lee happy. She had everything to give him, and he had so little to give her in return.

With Deanie Webber on one side of him and Mindy Jenkins on the other, he was caught in the middle of their giggling conversation. The moment he saw his sister go into the kitchen, he realized her departure gave him a means of escape.

"If you ladies will excuse me, I think Eve needs my help in the kitchen."

As much as he liked both Deanie and Mindy, a little bit of their bubbly personalities went a long way. He smiled and spoke to several people who greeted him warmly as he made his way through the crowd. He stopped twice to shake hands, first with the mayor and then with Phil Webber's brother, Charles, a local contractor.

Rick shoved open the hinged swinging door to Eve's big, bright kitchen, but stopped dead still when he heard what his sister was saying.

"I'll never be able to thank you enough, Miss Birdie." Eve wrapped her arms around the elderly woman and hugged her lovingly. "None of this could have happened without you. We owe you so much."

"Nonsense, girl." Grasping Eve's hands, Birdie patted them affectionately. "I did what I wanted to do. I've always thought Rick was the only man meant for my Lori Lee. Do you honestly think that I'd have let anything interfere with their happiness when they were finally so close to getting together?''

"Rick's like a new man since he got the loan. I've never seen him so happy, and with so many plans for the future. All his dreams are coming true, thanks to you.''

"All I did was make a phone call to my nephew over at Tuscumbia Savings and Loan,'' Birdie said.

Rick's jaw tightened painfully as he clamped his teeth together. He should have known. Dammit! He should have known! He'd been so proud of himself for getting the loan, so sure that the bank had given him the money he needed because of his personal credentials, his good credit report and his outstanding work record.

But it was a lie. All of it was a lie. What had Aunt Birdie done, guaranteed his loan with her own money? Yeah, that's exactly what she'd done. She wanted to make sure Lori Lee's future husband got what he needed to succeed in Tuscumbia, and the old woman sure as hell had enough money and clout to pull it off. Was that why so many of Tuscumbia's solid citizens were befriending him now? Why so many fellow businessmen attended the ribbon-cutting today and were here at this party tonight? Because Birdie Pierpont had issued an order requiring their presence?

Lori Lee had known, of course. Hell, she'd probably been the one to ask for her aunt's help. She knew he couldn't succeed on his own, that he didn't have a prayer of being accepted in this town without a great deal of help from someone with a whole lot of power. Lucky for her, she just happened to have an aunt who filled the bill.

"Let me add my thanks to my sister's,'' Rick said, his voice cold and deadly controlled.

Birdie gasped. Eve jumped. And the two women swung around guiltily, like two children caught with their hands in the cookie jar.

"Rick, don't get upset.'' Eve held out her hand pleadingly. "All Miss Birdie did was lean the scales back in your favor after all the harm Mara Royce and Powell Goodman caused."

"Is that what you did, Aunt Birdie? Lean the scales in my favor?" Rick glared at the old woman who lifted her double chin and stared at him defiantly. "Lori Lee said, Rick needs a big loan, Auntie. How about making sure he gets it?"

"That's not how it happened," Birdie told him.

"Isn't it?" Rick balled his hands into fists, longing to ram them through the wall. "You could've just given me the money outright. Why bother with the pretense of a loan? No, you couldn't do that, could you? Lori Lee probably told you that y'all would have to be careful not to bruise my ego and wound my pride. Better let Rick think he did this all on his own. That way he won't feel like he's been bought and paid for."

"Rick, how dare you say such a stupid thing to Miss Birdie," Eve scolded her brother.

"Yeah, how dare I? Especially after all she's done for me."

"Young man, you're sadly mistaken if you believe we plotted a conspiracy behind your back or if you think Lori Lee—"

The kitchen door swung open. "Are y'all in here talking about me?" With sparkling eyes and a wide smile on her face, Lori Lee glided into the kitchen. She slipped her arm around Rick's waist. He tensed at her loving touch. "What's wrong?"

Withdrawing from her embrace, he took a couple of steps away from her, then focused his dark gaze on her suddenly pale face.

"Rick overheard a private conversation and misunderstood something Eve and I were discussing," Birdie told her niece.

"What did Rick misunderstand?" Lori Lee posed the

question to her aunt, but her gaze never left Rick's stern face.

"Rick didn't misunderstand a damn thing," he said, then grabbed Lori Lee's arm. "You couldn't let me do it on my own, could you? You knew a loser like me could never succeed without a little help, so you got your aunt to fix things, to tidy up all my problems."

"What are you talking about?" Lori Lee stared at him, an incredulous look in her tear-glazed eyes. His fingers bit into her arm. She winced, but didn't cry out.

At that precise moment, Rick hated Lori Lee as much as he loved her. And yes, dammit all, he did love her. That had been another little bonus to his recent success. He'd finally gotten the courage and self-confidence to admit to himself that he had always loved Lori Lee Guy.

And she loved him—but not enough to accept him for the failure he was. No, she had to make sure she wasn't marrying some unacceptable loser.

"I'm talking about the fact that Aunt Birdie secured my loan with the bank. Hell, the money they loaned me probably came straight out of her account. But then you already know all about it, don't you, honey? You're the one I really have to thank for my business, for my new friends, for my acceptance by all the right people."

"Rick, you've got things wrong," Eve said. "You've blown the whole situation way out of proportion."

Jerking Lori Lee up against his hard chest, Rick narrowed his eyes and glowered at her, daring her to lie to him. "I wanted to do this on my own, dammit. You knew how important it was to me to prove myself. Maybe I couldn't have done it without your help, but this way it's meaningless."

Huge drops fell from Lori Lee's tear-filled eyes as she stared at Rick, her whole body slowly going numb. She reached down, prized his fingers from around her arm and took a faltering step backward. When he reached out to steady her, she slapped his hand, then turned and fled from the kitchen.

Birdie stomped her fat little foot on the floor. "Dammit, boy, you've gone and done it now."

"I wouldn't blame Lori Lee if she never forgives you for being such an idiot," Eve said.

"So this is all my fault?" Rick punched his chest with his index finger. "I'm the one that y'all made a fool of, you know. I'm the—"

"You, Rick Warrick, are a fool all right," Birdie told him. "But not for the reason you think. You just took out your anger on an innocent person."

A gnawing sense of fear ate away at Rick's stomach. "Are you trying to tell me that Lori Lee didn't mastermind this whole thing, that it wasn't her idea from the very beginning?"

"I'm telling you that there was no grand scheme for anyone to mastermind." Birdie waddled across the room and pointed her pudgy finger in Rick's face. "Eve told Lori Lee and me about your loan being turned down at Colbert Federal and the reason why." When Rick glared at Birdie, she nodded. "Yes, we both knew what had happened before you came by the shop that day."

"You'd already planned my rescue before I ever told Lori Lee anything," Rick accused her. "When she told me to apply for a loan at Tuscumbia Savings and Loan, she knew they wouldn't turn me down, didn't she?"

"Yes, she knew, just as I knew, that once they checked your records and saw that you qualified for the loan, they'd give it to you." Birdie shook her finger in his face. "And that's exactly the way it happened. You got the loan because you deserved it. Just like Darcie won her trophy because she deserved it."

"But you pulled some strings at the bank for me to get the loan," Rick said.

"All I did was call my nephew, Guy Stephenson, and tell him that when you applied for a loan, I wanted them to judge you on merit alone, and if they dared let John Hobart or Powell Goodman influence their decision in any way, I'd withdraw my money from their bank.'' Birdie tapped Rick on the chest several times, emphasizing her point. "I did just what Eve said I did, I tipped the scales back in your favor. You did the rest on your own."

"That's all you did?" Salty bile rose in Rick's throat. He suddenly felt sick at his stomach. God, he was a fool. And an idiot. And the biggest jerk in the world.

Tom Nelson swung open the kitchen door and walked in. "What's wrong with Lori Lee?" he asked. "She just ran out the front door and got in her car."

"She left?" Rick asked.

"Yeah, and she was in a pretty big hurry," Tom said. "I called out to her when I noticed she was crying, but I don't think she even heard me."

"I've got to go to her." Rick slammed his hand into the door, swinging it open.

Birdie grabbed his arm. "Don't you go to her unless you're prepared to do more than apologize to her. Don't go to her out of guilt and remorse. She deserves better."

"She deserves better than me," Rick agreed. "I've always known I wasn't good enough for her. But that's never stopped me from wanting her and it's not going to stop me from asking her to marry me."

Birdie loosened her hold on Rick, then patted his arm tenderly. "What Lori Lee needs is a man who will love her enough to overlook her flaws, to convince her that her inadequacies don't matter."

"That's the one thing I can give her. I can love her more than anybody else ever could."

"Can you love her despite her flaws?" Birdie asked.

"Lori Lee doesn't have any flaws," Rick said. "She's perfect. She's always been perfect."

"You're wrong, Rick. Lori Lee isn't perfect. No one is." Birdie looped her arm around Rick's. "I'll walk out to your truck with you. There's something I think you should know before you go after Lori Lee and ask her to marry you."

Rick pulled his truck up in the driveway directly behind Lori Lee's Riviera. When he reached the small porch of her two-story brick colonial house, he found the front door standing wide open.

Dear God, give me the chance to make things right with her. For once in my life, let me say and do all the right things. I can't blow this. I can't lose Lori Lee.

Walking into the foyer, Rick looked around, but didn't see her. He closed the door behind him.

"Lori Lee?"

Silence.

"Lori Lee, honey? Where are you?"

Silence.

"I know that I'm the biggest idiot in the world and you have every right not to forgive me, but if you'll just give me one more chance, I promise—"

"Don't make any promises you can't keep." Holding Tyke in her arms, Lori Lee walked out of the living room and halted in the doorway leading into the foyer.

"Honey, I..." He took a few tentative steps toward her, then held out his hands beseechingly. Her beautiful face was streaked with tears, her eyes red and swollen. He could kick himself for hurting her this way. "I acted like a macho jerk back at Eve's and I know it."

"You're a proud man." She stroked Tyke's head lovingly. "I realize that there have been times in your life that the only thing you had was your pride."

"Yeah, but in this case I let my pride get in the way of seeing the truth." Rick took another step toward her, holding his breath when she didn't back away from him. "Aunt Birdie and Eve set me straight. They've pretty much ripped all the hide off me, but you're welcome to rip off what's left."

Tyke squirmed in Lori Lee's arms. Leaning over, she set

him on the floor and patted his back. The little Boston terrier sniffed Rick's feet, then cocked his head and gave the big man a thorough inspection. Satisfied that their guest was friend and not foe, Tyke scurried off toward the living room.

Lori Lee straightened and looked at Rick, a tenuous smile on her lips. Fresh tears gathered in her eyes. "You can't spend the rest of your life afraid to believe in yourself. Darcie deserves a father who knows his own worth. How can you teach her to be self-confident, if you aren't?"

"What about you, Lori Lee? What do you deserve?" he asked, closing the gap between them with one final step.

When Rick reached out and tenderly clasped Lori Lee's elbows, she shivered as tears streamed down her cheeks. She shook her head, unable to answer his question.

"I'll tell you what you deserve." Rick bent down on one knee. "You deserve a man who loves you with all his heart and soul. A man who can promise to love you and be faithful to you for the rest of your life. A man who would lay down his life and die for you." Rick grabbled in his coat pocket for the jeweler's box. "A man who wants to spend the next fifty years or so doing everything he possibly can to make you happy."

Rick eased the jeweler's box from his pocket, lifted it in his hand and held it out as an offering. Lori Lee stared at the small velvet box, then looked down into Rick's dark eyes and saw tears.

"Oh, Rick."

He flipped open the box. Lori Lee gasped when she saw the golden topaz ring.

"I wish it could have been a big diamond," he said. "But when I saw this ring, I thought it looked like it belonged on your finger."

"It's beautiful. The most beautiful ring in the whole world."

Still on bended knee, Rick took her hand and slipped the

topaz on her finger. "Lori Lee Guy, I love you, more than anything. I want you to be my wife."

Falling to her knees, Lori Lee embraced him. "And I want to be your wife, but...but I can't. I can't marry you."

Rick lifted her to her feet, then took her in his arms and carried her into the living room. Laying her head on his shoulder, she clung to him when he sat down in the Queen Anne chair and placed her on his lap. Tyke scampered across the room and lay down at Rick's feet.

"Why can't you marry me?" he asked.

"I...there's something..." She gulped down the tears choking her. "I should have told you long ago, before you fell in love with me, before you—"

"There's something you should have told me fifteen years ago?" Caressing her cheek, he wiped away her tears with his big, rough fingertips.

"Fifteen years ago?" she gazed at him, her blue eyes questioning what he'd said.

"Yeah, that's when I fell in love with you. I didn't know it was love back then. All I knew was that I wanted you. But when I finally got around to admitting to myself that I was crazy in love with you, I realized that I've been in love with you all these years."

"Oh, Rick. Rick." She cupped his face in her hands and stared at him, all the love in her heart showing plainly in her eyes. "You fell in love with a dream, with a girl you thought was perfect. You still think I'm perfect, but I'm not."

"As far as I'm concerned you're perfect. My perfect woman."

Releasing his face, she grasped his shoulders and rested her forehead against his. Her body shook with the force of her sobs. "I—I'm not...not...perfect. I'm the most...most imperfect woman..."

Tilting her chin, he leaned over and kissed her forehead. "All right, honey, so you're an imperfect woman. That just makes you all the more perfect for an imperfect man like me.''

"No, Rick, you don't understand.'' She dug her nails into his shoulders. "I'm infertile. I can never give you a child.'' There, she'd finally been totally honest with him. Now that he knew the truth, he wouldn't want her.

"That's where you're wrong, honey. You've already given me a child,'' he told her.

"What? What did you say?'' Disbelief shone in her bright blue eyes.

"I already knew about your infertility before I proposed to you,'' Rick admitted. "Aunt Birdie told me, and she warned me to be damn sure and certain I loved you enough for your imperfection not to matter before I came over here.''

"You knew...before you... What did you mean about my already having given you a child?''

"All the way over here, while I was following you, I kept thinking about Darcie, about how much like you she is. And I don't mean just her blond hair and blue eyes. I'm talking about her talent and her personality and the pure sweet goodness in her.''

"Your wife. Your ex-wife. Darcie's mother was—''

"April Denton was a woman I picked up in a bar. The only similarity between you and her was the blond hair and blue eyes. Darcie is nothing like April. She's always looked more like you, been more like you, ever since she was a toddler. I used to look at her and wish she was our child.''

Lori Lee gasped again and again as she tried to control the torrent of tears engulfing her. She could not bear the pain, the hungry, helpless pain, inside her. Dear God in heaven, Darcie should have been her little girl. Hers and Rick's.

"Oh, baby, don't do this to yourself.'' Rick held her, caressing her, comforting her as she cried.

"Darcie should have been ours,'' Lori Lee said.

"She is ours, honey. That's what I'm trying to tell you.

Maybe April carried her in her body and gave birth to her, but she wasn't April's child. Not ever."

"I don't understand."

"The night I had sex with April, the only time I ever forgot to use protection, I thought she was you."

"You thought she was—"

"I'd been drinking, but I wasn't drunk," he said. "I picked April up in a bar because she reminded me a little bit of you. I was always finding girls with long blond hair and big blue eyes that reminded me of you. I suppose, in a way, every girl I was ever with was a substitute for you.

"What I'm trying to tell you, and doing a damn poor job of it, is that the night Darcie was conceived, I didn't make love to April. I didn't give her a child."

"Oh, Rick. Rick. You were—"

"Making love to you, Lori Lee. I was making love to you. Seven years ago on a hot August night in South Dakota, I was making love to you."

"Seven years ago? In August?" Lori Lee's thoughts drifted back to the last time she'd had sex with Tory, the night she had pretended he was Rick Warrick. "Oh, my God!"

"You knew, that night. Somehow you knew, didn't you, that I was making love to you?" Gripping her chin, he forced her to look at him. "Tell me, Lori Lee. Tell me!"

"In August, seven years ago, I—I suspected Tory was cheating on me, but I tried to convince myself he would never hurt me that way. It reached a point where I couldn't bear for him to touch me. The only way I could endure having sex with him was to—to—"

"To pretend he was me?"

"Yes. Yes."

"Don't you see, honey? The night Darcie was conceived, you and I were making love to each other. I didn't give April a child. I gave you a child. Darcie is the child of our love."

Lori Lee dissolved into a swirl of pain and joy, happiness

and grief, tears and sighs and boundless love. "Darcie's mine. My little girl." She kissed Rick's lips softly, tenderly. "Our little girl."

"Yeah, honey. Our little girl." He took her mouth in the sweetest, most powerful kiss they had ever shared. When he lifted his head, he smiled, tears streaming down his face. "Don't you think it's about time Darcie's parents got married."

"Yes. Yes, I do. I will. I..."

"And if you want more children, we'll find them. Kids nobody else wants. Kids like me. Bad boys trying to fight the world all alone."

"And kids like me," Lori Lee said. "Imperfect kids."

Rick stood with Lori Lee in his arms and carried her up the stairs to her bedroom. Tyke bounded up the steps behind them, then rushed ahead of them and curled up in a ball beside Lori Lee's bed.

There in the sweet darkness of night, they made love, committing their hearts and bodies to each other for a lifetime, and their souls to each other for all eternity.

Epilogue

A. K. Warrick, one of Tuscumbia's most successful businessmen and a recently elected city councilman, had been chosen as the grand marshal of the Helen Keller Festival parade. He and his family rode in the lead car, Rick's own classic 1956 blue-and-white Chevrolet convertible that he'd restored several years ago.

Lucie, their black-eyed, brown-haired four-year-old sat in her mother's lap. Although Lucie had been born deaf, she was a bright and beautiful child, who could sign quicker than most people could talk. Six-year-old Brandon, who suffered a mild form of cerebral palsy, had learned to take his first steps with the aid of a cane this year. The little towhead sat in Rick's lap and waved to the crowd every time his father waved.

Sitting proudly between his parents, thirteen-year-old Chris couldn't keep the smirky little grin off his face. Half the preteen girls, and a few teenage ones, were madly in love with Lori Lee's young heartbreaker. The first time she

saw Chris, she knew he was meant to be their child. He
acted so much like the old bad-boy Rick that he broke her
heart. He'd been an unwanted, unloved hellion who dared
anyone to care about him. Their friends warned them not
to adopt Chris. At eight he was already a hoodlum. But
Rick and Lori Lee could not resist the challenge, Rick
knowing better than anyone that love was the boy's only
hope. Now Chris was a popular, well-liked athlete and
honor-roll student.

When they rode by the studio, Aunt Birdie, who stood
on a stepladder so she could see over the crowd, waved her
pudgy hand. She was excited about this year's festivities
more so than any other year. Just in time for the annual
festival, the workers had completed renovations in the basement, restoring the Prohibition speakeasy to its former
glory. Birdie's Golden Cage, as she'd dubbed her pet project, had been listed on the tour of homes and local attrac-
tions. Where tourists would be greeted at every stop on the
tour by lovely young girls in antebellum costumes, they
were met at Birdie's by a roly-poly, white-haired femme
fatale in a black-and-red flapper costume.

The Dixie Twirlers, national and world champions,
marched behind the Deshler band. Deanie Webber had vol-
unteered to oversee their performance so that Lori Lee
could ride with Rick in the grand marshal's car.

The only member of the Warrick family not riding with
them was seventeen-year-old Darcie. As Deshler's head
majorette, like her mother before her, Darcie marched with
the band. Her best friend, Katie Webber, marched beside
her. The Warricks' oldest, who would be a high school
senior when school started in the fall, was already making
plans to follow in Lori Lee's footsteps and try out for the
majorette line at the University of Alabama.

Everyone who saw the beautiful mother and daughter
together marveled at their striking resemblance, and those
who personally knew them were constantly amazed at how
alike in personality and temperament the two were. But

Rick and Lori Lee weren't surprised. They knew that Darcie was their own special miracle.

Of course, all of the Warrick children were special miracles. Each had been destined to be a part of their warm, caring family and to grow up surrounded by the love of a reformed bad boy and a slightly imperfect Southern belle.

* * * * *

And the Winner Is...
You!

...when you pick up these great titles
from our new promotion at your
favorite retail outlet this June!

Diana Palmer
The Case of the Mesmerizing Boss

Betty Neels
The Convenient Wife

Annette Broadrick
Irresistible

Emma Darcy
A Wedding to Remember

Rachel Lee
Lost Warriors

Marie Ferrarella
Father Goose

This summer, the legend
continues in Jacobsville

A LONG, TALL
TEXAN SUMMER

Three **BRAND-NEW** short stories

This summer, Silhouette brings readers a special
collection for Diana Palmer's LONG, TALL TEXANS
fans. Diana has rounded up three **BRAND-NEW**
stories of love Texas-style, all set in Jacobsville,
Texas. Featuring the men you've grown to love from
this wonderful town, this collection is a must-have
for all fans!

*They grow 'em tall in the saddle in Texas—and
they've got love and marriage on their minds!*

Don't miss this collection of original Long, Tall Texans
stories...available in June at your favorite retail outlet.